HELL IN A HEAD GASKET

THE DEVIL'S DAUGHTER (BOOK 1)

G.A. CHASE

BAYOU MOON PRESS, LLC

ABOUT THIS BOOK

When Sere Mal-Laurette escaped hell, she thought she'd left her demons behind her. But now that one has found his way through hell's gate, others are sure to follow. Then all hell will break loose.

If Sere fails to contain the little soulless bastards, the loas of the dead will likely figure out her true identity. Then they'll be all over her soul, and she can kiss immortality goodbye. Moreover, someone needs to send the demons back to where they came from before they wreak havoc on the citizens of New Orleans.

To prevent the demon doppelgängers from killing their human equivalents and taking over their lives, Sere will need the help of people she trusts—and some she doesn't. It's time for her to embrace the badass demon hunter she was always meant to be. To do so, however, she'll have to quickly figure out the line between protector of humanity and murdering psychopath.

1

---

*H*igh above the murky swamp waters, Sere Mal-Laurette lay naked in the porch hammock, watching the sun set over the bayou. It wasn't the peaceful end of the day, however, that held her attention. The green glow on the horizon that she hoped she was just imagining grew brighter as the light of day faded. She rolled over toward the decrepit cabin nestled in the limbs of the cypress tree.

"It's probably just a chemical-plant fire or distant lightning strikes." She knew in her gut, however, that her plausible explanations were nothing more than a desire to turn her back on her obligation. The same burst of Day-Glo green had heralded her crossing between dimensions.

She bolted out of the woven-rope cocoon like a scalded cat and stood with fists clenched at the railing. "Damn it! The gate to hell isn't a revolving door. Why can't you demons leave me alone? I didn't make my escape just to have you fools follow me like I was some demented Pied Piper of the damned." No one would be able to hear her on the island far out in the swamp, but yelling provided a release, however brief, to her frustration.

Though corralling the recently escaped soulless demon back into its dimension wasn't her responsibility, she sure as hell would pay the price if its existence among the living was discovered. The voodoo loas of the dead were on constant guard against empty bodies. Sere—as a soul stolen from Guinee, placed in one of those empty shells, and made immortal—was number one on their Most Wanted list. So long as they believed the gate between realms was sealed with their missing soul trapped inside, they had no reason to suspect it was she, and not her father, who had sidestepped the final resting place. One dumb-ass demon flailing around life like a drunken college student on spring break would make the loas leave their realm to start investigating.

With no choice but to search for the cause of the rift, she stared into the bayou, trying to estimate the green glow's location. Between the meandering rivers, cypress groves, and hyacinth-clogged marshes, finding her way directly through the swamp would be impossible. Like an ever-changing maze, hell's swamp never provided the same connection between dimensions twice.

She clenched her fists so hard her fingernails bit into her palms. "Fuck. It's not likely the demon will just be sitting out there waiting for me. I might work my way out there just to find out the fucker has already made it into some hick town. The more attention it attracts, the sooner the loas will be all over my ass."

The only way to discover what dangers lay ahead was to follow the path behind her—the one leading away from the peace of her swamp cabin and back to the chaos of towns filled with people. If something strange had slithered, swum, flown, or walked out of the bayou, it would certainly be the talk of the superstitious redneck bar gossips. All she had to do was wander the small taverns, getting hit on by fat assholes with missing teeth, until she found one drunk enough to think he had a shot at impressing a passing young woman with his tales of derring-do.

"No point in dragging this out." She entered the cabin that had been her home in both hell and life for nineteen of her twenty-six years of existence. The place still reeked of spells cast by the original swamp witch, hell's creator, to contain Sere's father. *Too bad Agnes Delarosa sucked so badly at containment charms.* Even though the old witch was long gone, some ideas were best left unspoken.

Sere squeezed into the skintight black leather pants and matching halter top. Once her body adjusted to the outer coverings, the outfit moved like a second skin. She sat in the dusty rocking chair that Agnes's granddaughter, Sanguine Delarosa, had used to cradle Sere in as a young child. The alligator-skin boots she yanked on fit snugly over the riding pants.

Before climbing down from the porch, she stepped on the lower board of the railing and reached down to her boot. The combat knife was sheathed inside just as she'd expected, but touching the handle of the deadly weapon gave her a sense of reassurance. It and the clothes on her back were all she needed from the cabin. She'd snatch whatever else she required from the hidden cache close to the highway.

She looked back at the open door, wondering if she should lock the place up. "If anyone stumbles this far out and needs a place to hole up, I expect something like a rusty lock won't prove much of an obstacle. Besides, what is there worth stealing?"

The dark of night was fast approaching. While most people headed to the safety of their homes, Sere would start her hunt, but first, she needed transportation. She climbed down the makeshift ladder consisting of a dozen boards nailed to the tree trunk. Then, with all the enthusiasm of a commuter facing a wearisome drive to work the nightshift, she approached the weathered canoe tied up in the reeds. With a firm push, she had the fiberglass hull off the silt bank and into the dark water. As she jumped in and pulled away from the island, she watched the last rays of daylight brighten the storm-tossed cabin like a beacon to help her find her way home.

~

AFTER AN HOUR of paddling along the well-known waterways, Sere beached the old canoe on an island that looked like every other one she'd passed. Headlights from cars plying the interstate a half mile away barely illuminated the old shipping container that lay on its side, covered in vines. "Let's see what surprises you have for me this time."

Strictly speaking, the cache wasn't hers. Joe Cazenave was a firm believer in having escape options, and for every covert store of supplies, he had constantly changing security features. As her fighting instructor and mentor, he seldom complained when Sere borrowed what she needed. However, that didn't mean she didn't have to figure out his deadly little puzzles to gain access.

She squatted down to begin her inspection of the rust-red garage-sized metal strongbox. It had sunk low enough into the bog that a small moat had formed around it like a medieval castle. Based on the flat rock wedged against the container's top—now facing sideways—and the matching one meant to look haphazardly buried in the reeds, she assumed the protective guardians Joe had assigned to keep an eye on his treasures weren't fluffy little river otters.

She thought back to her training. Joe set up his caches such that even if he turned up naked and near death, he could still open the box. "Everything I need is right in front of me." The jump from rock to slippery moss-covered rock would be a challenge even in the best of conditions. "There must be a makeshift bridge somewhere close."

A little hunting through the vines and reeds revealed the waterlogged plank. After setting it over the two rocks, she carefully edged her way to the center of the protective canal. A ball of water moccasins teemed so tightly under her feet that she wondered if the head of Medusa was buried in the silt.

"Clever, Joe." Even if some kid did happen upon the treasure chest, he wouldn't risk multiple snakebites just to explore an abandoned shipping container. But the snakes would only be Joe's first line of defense.

Sere didn't even bother working her way toward the front to check the bolted-shut doors. They would be much too obvious for a man trained in all manner of military evasion tactics. The rock under the board hadn't sunk at all from her crossing. She bounced on her toes to make sure of its stability. "You wouldn't have bothered with a foundation unless you knew it would be needed." Staring up along the corrugated metal, she caught sight of a rust-free section of the top surrounded by thick vines. "Right."

Even if Joe had shown up in a bad way, the ability to run up a wall was so firmly ingrained in his conditioning that he'd have had no problem performing the basic-training maneuver. Like a military cadet, Sere backed up to the far side of the plank and took a running start at the rusty-metal climbing wall. Her smooth boots slipped on the wet wood and metal as she leaped high enough to grasp the thick creepers that hung off the cabinet. Hand over hand, she pulled her slender frame up onto the top of the shipping container.

From above the marsh, she could barely make out the circuitous route from the island to the mainland. "You never could make anything easy, could you, Joe?"

A passing set of misaligned truck headlights made her hit the deck to avoid any possibility of being seen. Lying flat on the box, she ran her hand over a section of repaired corrugated metal. It had been aged to look no different from the rest of the container, but based on the Phillips-head screws, she knew she'd discovered Joe's way in.

No matter how clever you think you are, never accept your first—or even your hundredth—conclusion that you are safe. Joe's words were like an encyclopedia of self-doubt. His puzzles were bomb-disposal chess matches.

She ran her fingertip around the head of the nearest screw. As with the front door, simply using it as intended was far too obvious. "If I'm not supposed to turn you, then what am I to do with you, little fucker?"

A sliver of metal that had gotten trapped under the screw head sliced into her finger. "Ouch." Sere put her fingertip to her mouth. The metallic taste of blood made her realize the cut hadn't been accidental. She pulled her finger out of her mouth and squeezed it until a drop of blood formed. Then she dripped it into the indented cross of the screw head. The plate of repaired steel popped up just enough for her to work her fingers underneath. "DNA detector... you're getting technological on me, old man."

The hidden door lifted up like the hood of a car. She scampered under the steel plate and landed on the floor like a cat jumping off a ledge. Once the secret hatch had reclosed, lights came on in the shipping container.

The contents made her smile. "Joe's garage." As a combination of fallout shelter, resupply depot, and workshop, the room was filled with food, weapons, tools, and—most importantly—four motorcycles, which stood proudly along the wall. Her packed alligator saddlebags—made from the same hide as her boots—were secured on the back of a vintage Triton. The handmade café racer made up of a Triumph motor mounted into a Norton frame was so well constructed that she knew it must have been one of

Joe's creations. "Is there anything you can't do with your hands?"

A note taped to the gas cap read, "throttle sticks, no rev limiter." She wasn't sure if the message indicated further work he intended to do, a warning to Sere, or intentional modifications. The leather bomber jacket draped over the handlebars was a nice touch. She threw it on. Based on how tightly if fit around her chest and shoulders, she had to wonder which of his conquests had left it behind.

"Let's hear how you sound." She threw her leg over the seat and gave the starter a firm thrust. The old engine kicked over but grumpily refused to start. "I see how it is. Just like your creator—as obstinate as hell." She stood the bike up off its kickstand, jumped six inches into the air, and landed with the full force of her five-foot, four-inch, one-hundred-three-pound frame against the foot lever. The bike roared to life like an English lion.

Before coaxing the motorcycle toward the main doors, Sere enviously eyed the wall lined with knives, guns, and explosives. She resisted the temptation. "No point in stealing anything else until I know what I'm up against. Best to travel light."

For a normally high-revving speedster, the Triton crept along the metal floor like a wild cat controlling its desire to pounce. When the front tire hit the ramp five feet from the rusted-shut doors, hydraulic rams lowered the wall like the opening to Batman's cave. The heavy metal plate fell across the swamp moat, creating a drawbridge.

Halfway across, Sere stopped and set the bike on its kickstand. She stared over the edge at the water teeming with snakes. "I suppose a little company for my personal protection wouldn't hurt. It's not like a couple of you guys would take up much room in my bags." As she lowered her hands into the water, the water serpents gathered around them, each vying to be plucked out of the moat. She chose two young and energetic canebrake rattlesnakes. They wriggled around her wrists until she fed their heads into the top flaps of her saddlebags. Their thin, scaly bodies disappeared into the darkness with only a final shake of their rattles as thanks for being included in the upcoming adventure. With living companions from the swamp she loved, heading out into the wilds of humanity felt slightly less daunting.

2

*S*ere shut down her Triton in front of Bubba's Bar and Grill. After two hours straddling the high-vibration engine, she was ready for a shot and a fight—preferably in that order. The row of Harley Davidsons that took up prime real estate on either side of the front door displayed their asses to her like an aging chorus line. Not one of the bikes was less than thirty years old, and more than a few looked like they'd been ridden hard for too long. *At least I won't be dealing with rich-kid wannabe bikers,* she thought.

She swung her leg off the tandem seat and unbuckled her skullcap helmet. Dust from the gravel parking lot, kicked up by her tires, hung thick in the humid night air. She tossed her leather helmet onto the matching saddlebags and left the petcock under the gas tank set to open. "I won't be long."

At some point in the building's history, someone must have thought old-West-style swinging front doors gave a bar some panache. Really, the only thing the squeaky hinges and banging doors were useful for was announcing any new patron's arrival. She scanned the bar for both potential threats and tactical advantages. She had the room mapped out before the hinges of the swinging door stopped their screeching.

Four guys playing pool. All holding their sticks like boners and, just like their cocks, easily neutralized. Fat fuck at the end of the bar—I expect he's the rider of the worn-out-suspension Wide Glide closest to the front door. Loud asshole arguing with waitress. He's more bluster than brawn, but the girl could be an issue. From the muscles she's displaying under her tank top, she clearly could put him in his place without saying a word, but she is doing a masterful job of controlling her irritation. Bartender has a Navy SEAL tattoo on his bulging bicep that he's only half hiding under a sweaty T-shirt. Must remember not to turn my back on that one.

She took a seat on the swivel barstool. *One good kick to the chair's base, and it will separate to provide me with a useful shield.*

The bartender leaned an elbow on the cypress counter. "What can I get ya, pretty lady?"

Smooth talker. He's sizing me up, but as a threat or a conquest? "Shot of Jameson."

He tapped on the bar with his knuckles as if recording the drink order on the polished wood.

"Hey, is it true that gingers don't have souls?" Fat Fuck

asked. He apparently thought insulting a woman made for a good pickup line.

"I don't know," Sere replied. "Is it true fat pricks can't see their dicks? Tell me, how exactly do you get it on with a woman? Does she have to be bowlegged? Because the basic geometry eludes me."

"You've got quite the mouth on you, little girl." The barstool groaned under his weight as he turned toward her.

Bartender Smooth slid the shot to Sere but addressed Fat Fuck. "No need for that."

The tub of flesh returned to his drink. "If the little girl can't take some ribbing, maybe she shouldn't frequent bars."

"Sounds to me like she was simply giving back what you were serving up." Bartender Smooth turned back to Sere and used his well-worn dishrag to polish up a glass beer stein. "You from around here or just passing through?"

Wonderful. We're at the brass-tacks-disguised-as-small-talk section of the evening. Sere hated casual conversations, but she needed to get someone to start talking. Bartender Smooth seemed like the type of dude who would hit on every woman who strayed into his domain. Having asshole customers made him appear the white knight out to rescue any damsel stupid enough to be distressed by the bar's clientele. At least the lothario might be a little freer with information than the rest of the bikers. "A little of both. I'm doing some research on the swamp's mythical creatures. Have you heard of any strange things happening out on the water or know of any available johnboats for hire?"

From his condescending look, she half expected some

crack about her being a rich college student seeking adventure. "People are always asking about the rougarou wolf," he said, "or the Fifolet pirate ghost or the Pleistocene gator. Just stories to sell swamp tours to unsuspecting tourists, in my opinion. But if you're looking to tool around the swamp for an hour or two during the day, I'm sure I can set you up with a boat and captain happy to take your money." The man's head remained aimed at her as his eyes flashed around the room so discreetly Sere nearly missed his assessment. The man's tattoo wasn't just for show. Military training was hard to acquire and impossible to hide. "However, if you're looking for anything more than the typical tour of the swamp, you should know that gator hunters don't take kindly to strangers scoping out their grounds."

"Thanks for the warning. What I'm seeking is deep in the bayou, beyond the alligator-hunting grounds. I doubt I could reach the area in a few hours. I'm not looking for a guide, only the use of a boat for a few days."

He finally set the glass on the shelf. "Horror stories aside, no one stays out in the swamp after dark. Even the best of navigators can get lost in the myriad waterways, and no one wants to get stuck out there without help. Plus, when it comes to catching gators, a hunter can lose his tags if he's not off the water by sunset. The state's pretty strict about such things. Even if you could find someone willing to rent you a boat, they'd never agree to more than a couple of hours. Maybe you should consider a safer line of research."

Fat Fuck slid his empty beer glass down the bar. It nearly careened into Sere's hand. "I could show you a thing or two that would make you quiver. The bayou ain't no place for a little girl all alone."

Call me little girl one more time, and I'll knock some of that fat off of your lard ass. "I was raised by a swamp witch, so nothing out there frightens me." She eyed his fat belly, which hung over the front of the barstool. "And I highly doubt there's anything you could show me that I'd find impressive. As for your hunting grounds, they might as well be kiddy fishing ponds at the state fair as far as I'm concerned." She leaned against the stool's short back and kicked her boots onto the counter in front of Bartender Smooth for the man's inspection, discreetly placing the one with the knife on the bottom. "You sound like you know your river animals. Tell me what you see."

He ran his hands over the two-inch-diameter ridged scales that covered Sere's foot. "Big horny scutes, aren't they? From the umbilical scar on the boot's upper, the hide is clearly from an alligator, but not like one I've ever run across. The leather is softer than most gator hides—nearly that of a saltie. Those shoes must have cost you a pretty penny." Though his hands stopped at the top of the scaled leather, his eyes continued considerably higher up her legs.

She yanked the gator-skin boots off the bar. "She was my pet. When she died, I skinned her, tanned her, and made these boots."

A roar of laughter indicated that every person in the bar had been paying attention. "Listen here, little girl. If you're gonna tell a whopper, at least make it believable." Fat Fuck's speech was so filled with saliva that Bartender Smooth had to wipe down the bar with his rag.

She hooked the toe of her boot under the foot ring of the barstool. "Are you calling me a liar?"

Bartender Smooth slid another beer toward Fat Fuck. "Let's keep it civilized. I don't need another bar fight, especially when the provocateur is so outnumbered."

Loud Mouth leaned back in his chair and spread his legs as if he was trying to display his junk. "So all this talk of women's liberation ends when things get physical? That doesn't sound right. Any other biker that set foot in this bar and lied through their teeth would face a proper whooping."

Damn it. A few more minutes, and I might have learned something useful about the swamp. She downed the second shot of Jameson that Bartender Smooth had set in front of her like a peace offering. "I was just looking for some information."

The four dudes at the pool table circled in toward her like sharks sensing blood. "You were looking to horn in on our swamp land. I don't know how you heard about the monster gator being on our lands, but any creature that valuable belongs to us." The tallest of the four punctuated his words with flicks of his cue.

Damn it, Lefty. I told you to stay in the deep swamp. With the sound of the pool stick being snapped in half, Sere knew the time for polite conversation had come to an end. She hurled the empty shot glass at Fat Fuck's eye and clocked him so perfectly that the ton of flesh fell off his chair and shook the floor. *One down.*

By launching backward off her barstool, she was able to swing its base up with her foot. With one good yank of the seat cushion, the heavy cast-iron base came free. She grabbed the shaft in midflight and twirled the lattice ironwork like a parasol. The first pool dude lunged with his broken stick like some foolish kid trying to poke a hornet's nest. Sere caught the splintered end with her rotating iron-lattice disk and wrenched it out of his grasp so forcefully she felt his shoulder dislocate.

The rest of the mob closed in fast. With one complete swing of the heavy iron, she not only cleared an opening around her but also built up momentum. Laying the base back on the floor, she transferred the centrifugal force into linear projection and launched into the air like a circus acrobat. She caught Loud Mouth smack in the jaw with her knee as she flew over his head, causing him to fall backward and crush the chair behind him. She reached out and did a hand flip off the neighboring table.

Like a swimmer doing a kick turn, she hit the back wall with her feet and barreled back toward the crowd. With her arms set like a flying cross, she wiped out two more of the pool players, but the reduced momentum landed her on the floor. She scampered up with her back against the bar just as the final pool player made a mad rush at her. He stopped cold like a cartoon character who'd just realized his mistake when he found the tip of her knife at his throat.

"I didn't come here looking for trouble," she said.

The cold steel circles of a double-barreled shotgun pressed under Sere's hair at the back of her skull. "Oh, I'll bet trouble just follows you around like a lovesick puppy. Hand over the knife."

Fuck. I knew better than to turn my back on Bartender Smooth. She reached back and set the blade on the bar.

The final pool dude's smile revealed missing teeth. "Now we're gonna have a little fun."

From behind him, the waitress wacked the dude in the head with an empty beer bottle like she was swatting a fly. He went down hard. "Don't get any crazy idea about female unity," the waitress said, "but no woman should have to endure Leroy's brand of flirting."

The gun was still pointed at Sere's head while the injured started finding their way back to their feet. Things were about to get ugly.

"This looks like a Ranger's knife," Bartender Smooth said. "Not many of those show up on the open market. I'd wager you picked it up at the same place as those boots."

"It was given to me by a friend." *Who also taught me how to use it.*

In front of her, the group was forming into a lynch mob. The gun barrel behind her shifted as the bartender picked up the knife. *This is it.* She swung around to her left, forcing the barrel away from her head. Instinctively, Bartender Smooth pulled the trigger. The unintended shotgun blast of rock salt cleared the most aggressive of Sere's pursuers. She caught the hot metal barrel in her armpit and kept spinning to force the gun out of Bartender Smooth's hands. With one swing of the empty weapon, she cleared enough of a path to bolt for the door. She busted through the swinging gate and was on the back of her bike before the others had a chance to regroup.

∽

SERE GAVE one good kick of the starter and had the Triton roaring to life. Gunning the throttle, she peppered the other motorcycles with gravel from her rear tire before finding traction on the narrow lane of pavement that stretched out of town. Like a racehorse let out of the gate, the motorcycle settled back on its rear shocks and tore off down the road.

The others weren't far behind. If her café racer took to the chase like a thoroughbred, the heavy Harleys acted like Clydesdales hammering the asphalt, making far more noise than speed. Within a mile, the thunderous roar of the manly V-twins had died down to a pathetic whimper on the breeze. But as Sere left the heavy cruisers in the dust, the ominous howl of a high-performance Ducati grew in intensity.

Fuck a Duc. Sere leaned low across the curved gas tank to cut down on wind resistance and gave her bike every bit of throttle it could handle. She'd never be able to outrun or outmaneuver the monster on her tail. She needed to think fast if she didn't want to end up as roadkill. *I didn't see that bike when I left the bar. It must be Bartender Smooth's ride. He'd likely have the speed demon parked out back and aimed at the road for a quick pursuit. I need to stop underestimating that dude.*

She downshifted and made a quick right-hander onto a gravel road to get off the even pavement. Hopefully, the guy on her ass would have enough love for his crotch rocket to avoid having it pelted with rocks. Gunning the engine, she raised a cloud of pebbles and dust with her tires to make the narrow path as uninviting as possible.

But the high-pitched howl grew louder.

Damn you. Why can't you take no for an answer? Just like a redneck. Think, girl. How do I dump this dumb-ass suitor? She scanned the dark path ahead with little optimism. The sound of chainsaws, smell of freshly cut lumber, and intense glare of high-wattage floodlights broke the heavy vegetation to her left. *At least I'm not alone,* she thought, though she suspected the biker dudes back at the bar had friends among the night road crew. *I'll have to risk it.*

She swung her bike down the first heavily wheel-rutted logging road she came to. A semi with its windshield caked with dust blasted an irate air horn at her impudence. The screeching of the big truck's brakes was sure to alert ol' Smoothie of her maneuver. With barely enough room to squeeze by, she angled her bike between the truck trailer's massive iron brackets—which were loaded down with tree trunks—and the roadbed. Peering through the undergrowth, she saw the bulk of the road-building equipment in a holler below. The shallow land formation cleared of vegetation looked as though a giant had used a spoon to scoop out the center of a mound of mashed potatoes, complete with a gravy-mud lake in the middle. *Perfect.*

Instead of sticking to the truck route that skirted the rim of the holler, she aimed her bike along a dried-out streambed that snaked over the edge into the valley. She only had to maintain her grasp of her bucking machine for a hundred feet as the narrow tires hit every rock and rut before she came on the access road that paralleled the logging road she'd left. Rather than continuing in front of the pursuing bike, she turned into the path of the rider above. Staying low and sticking close to the wall of the ravine so as not to be seen, she made as much noise as possible.

From the other side of the bowl-shaped canyon, she caught the familiar sound of her valiant Triton engine echoing off the bare cliff opposite the direction she was headed. If Bartender Smooth was relying on what he heard, he'd believe she'd just darted well ahead of him but that he was still tracking her in the right direction. From the roadway above, the engine howl transitioned to a piston-driven scream. *Apparently, Smoothie doesn't take rejection well.*

She continued tearing up the dirt-and-gravel road until the sound of the Ducati was just a distant angry buzz. It wasn't until she'd returned to the well-paved road heading away from Bubba's Bar that she realized the hot moisture that wetted her inner calf wasn't the result of her exertion. One touch to the thick oil confirmed her worst fear. *Fucking head gasket.* Like a bad dog satisfying himself on her leg, the Triton was spewing hot fluid all over her leather pants. She let off the throttle and pulled in the clutch to coast the bike down the long, winding road into the next town.

THE BIKE'S momentum only took her as far as Kelly's Diner, at the outskirts of the small hamlet. Sere eyed a weathered gray pickup truck out front with Big Larry's Machine Shop painted on the cab door. She hoped Big Larry wasn't another fucking biker.

Sere appreciated the bonding experience people felt when sharing a meal, as if they were saying, *We're all human.*

We've all gotta eat. Of course, as a resident of hell's dimension, that wasn't strictly true for her. But she had to admit, a good cup of coffee and a slice of warm pie were about the best experiences life had to offer, even if the sustenance was only for show.

She rummaged through her saddlebag for a fresh pair of jeans and underwear. The two-foot-long rattlesnake curled up her arm. "I don't have time to play right now. Stay on guard in case someone tries something funny." She peeled the body-heat-loving serpent off her arm and coiled it back on top of her undies.

As she walked into the diner, she performed her usual scan of customers, potential threats, and possible improvised weapons. Unlike the bar, the diner's booths were filled with happy families and the counter lined with overweight customers enjoying dinner, which didn't present much of a concern. She stood in front of the Wait to Be Seated sign while a scrawny little fella in coveralls paid his tab at the register.

The matronly woman behind the counter flashed Sere a welcoming smile. "I'll be right with you, hon."

The guy paying his bill pulled cash out with his grease-smudged hands. "Thanks for the grub, Kelly."

"Same time tomorrow, Larry? I'll have a fresh batch of apple pies for dinner."

"Yummy." As he turned toward Sere, she read the shop label on his blue-and-white-striped coveralls: Big Larry's.

"You wouldn't happen to be the guy with the machine shop, would you?" she asked.

"That's me. From the look of your pants, I guess you might be in need of some help."

Sere made another scan of the restaurant to make sure there wasn't a much bigger Larry Senior lurking in the bathroom hallway. "Are you the owner?" she asked dubiously.

His low-pitched single chuckle sounded well rehearsed. "I get that a lot. Either I can have a look at your problem while you change clothes, or you can join me while I tell you my life's story. Your choice."

Kelly reached out for Sere's change of attire. "You can leave those here if you want, hon. Larry will have your motor diagnosed in far less time than it will take you to clean up. He's too kind to tell you he's in a hurry, even though he always is. I swear that guy lives in his workshop. While you're out there, I'll find you a bar of grease-cutting soap and some wash rags."

Sere handed over her fresh jeans with underwear wrapped inside. "Thanks."

Larry held the door open for Sere, though whether out of chivalry or a desire to keep his favorite dining spot oil free, she couldn't tell. The slick that enveloped her leg seemed to be spreading like swamp mange.

"What seems to be the problem?" he asked.

She cocked her ear down the two-lane highway, fearful of hearing the roar of motorcycle engines. "My bike blew a head gasket."

Larry let out a long whistle at the sight of the motorcycle half-coated in oil. "I would say so. Haven't seen a café racer like this in a coon's age."

In light of her recent run-in, she couldn't ignore the danger of being caught by some associate of the beer-loving biker gang. "I suppose you mostly get Harleys in your shop."

His chuckle sounded far more genuine this time. "Want to guess why they call me Big Larry?"

She shrugged at his non-sequitur question. "My first guess was that the shop name referred to your father."

He knelt down next to the bike for a better look at the problem. "Nope. My dad was a loudmouth good-for-nothing drunk. As a kid, I got picked on by damn near everyone. They used to call me Runt. A girl I knew started calling me Big Larry to get the assholes off my back. Since I'm clearly diminutive in stature, we left it to their sexually charged diminished mental capacities to figure out what she was referring to."

This time it was Sere's turn to chuckle. "But surely they must have caught on when they saw you in the gym showers."

"This was in elementary school. With my friend's help, I quickly developed a reputation for being a lady's man. Being seen as the first out of the puberty blocks gave me enough of a head start that no one questioned my nickname later in life. The assholes that used to call me Runt all ride Harleys now, so you can imagine not many of them turn to me when they need repairs."

Sere breathed a little easier hearing that Larry wouldn't be the one to betray her to the biker gang. She leaned down next to him beside the bike. "So is this something you can fix?"

"Oh, sure. I can get the engine apart tonight. I'll have to

send to Baton Rouge for the parts. If I get the order in early tomorrow morning, I should get what I need by late afternoon. I should have you back on the road by Wednesday morning. Are you staying in town? Kelly has some short-term-rental rooms available."

Sere looked down the main street, wondering who would possibly be looking for an Airbnb so far from civilization. "Is her cooking really so good it attracts tourists?"

Larry lowered his head to hide his laugh. "You'll never catch me saying anything but praises about that woman. She's the one that gave me my nickname. However, I've yet to meet anyone who came to town for one of her meals. Mostly she rents to city dudes out here for a gator adventure tour. The bayou docks are about a half mile down that side road."

Perfect. With the confirmation from the drunks at Bubba's that there was still something lurking in the swamp, she needed a way to sneak out there without drawing further attention. Lefty wouldn't risk his alligator hide unless he was trying to draw her attention. "Since I'll only need a spot to toss my bedroll for two nights, I'll make my own arrangements."

"Suit yourself." He pulled out a work-order notebook from his overalls. "How about a number where I can reach you?"

She took the pad and scribbled down the number Joe had given her in case of emergencies. "This will get you in touch with Joe Cazenave. He'll take care of the expenses."

Larry looked at her with half-closed, suspicious eyes. "So

you won't give out your phone number, aren't willing to let me know where you're staying, and wanted to make sure I was on the level. You on the run from someone, pretty lady?"

Though at every moment, she feared hearing a motorcycle engine from down the road, and though she could use an ally, letting on about her situation to a stranger would be a tactical mistake that would earn her a hard glare from Joe. "Not enough to pass up on one of Kelly's world-famous pies."

"*Parish famous* maybe. I know enough about women to know when not to push. Give me a hand, and we'll get your bike loaded into my truck. When it comes time to pick up your ride, my shop is at the other end of town. You can't miss it."

Once the bike was loaded and strapped down, she pulled her saddlebags off the back and bedroll off the front fender. Seeing Larry pull away with the Triton was like watching a doctor wheel a relative into surgery. *Don't be stupid. It's just a bike.*

～

SERE DRAPED her red-and-white-checkered napkin over the remaining crumbs of her rhubarb pie. Cleaned up and well fed, she did her best to not appear suspicious as she glanced out the side windows of Kelly's Diner. *It's been over an hour. Each of those dicks is probably back at the bar, licking his wounded pride—or changing the story to make himself out as the victor. Either way, I can't imagine any of those lazy fucks lasting this long on their loud-exhaust bikes. All roar and no stamina, just like their riders.*

"Can I get you anything else, hon?" Kelly stood next to the table. Her quick glance to see what Sere had been focusing on made Sere believe the woman wasn't just referring to what was on the menu.

"I think I'm fine."

Kelly flipped the order form closed and put it back in the pocket of her apron. "The meal is on me tonight. What should I say if anyone comes looking for you?"

You don't miss much, do you? Sere thought. "As little as possible."

"You were never here. I'll pass the word to Larry as well, though most people in this town underestimate his observational abilities. Are you sure you won't take up my offer of a clean, safe place to sleep?"

The notion that being inside somehow equaled being safe had long baffled Sere. "You've already been more than generous."

Kelly continued looking around the diner as if making sure they weren't overheard. "I know the signs of domestic abuse when I see them—fresh bruises, constantly checking every face you see, not trusting anyone, and traveling without much more than the clothes on your back. I also know when someone's not comfortable accepting help." She slid a small stack of twenty-dollar bills under Sere's napkin. "If you have to stay on the run, you'll probably need a little cash." Sere tried to object, but Kelly put her hand on Sere's shoulder before she could get the words out. "Whatever you were about to say, you can just stuff it.

Stay here as long as you feel safe. I'll bring you a fresh iced tea."

Sere kicked the saddlebags and bedroll at her feet. "If I do end up sneaking out, would you mind stashing my things until I come back for my bike?"

"Of course, hon." As the overly caring woman moved on to the next table, Sere pocketed the money. *Never know when it might come in handy.*

She sat nursing her continually filled iced tea until she saw dented trucks with mud-covered wheels and fenders—complete with alligator blood dripping from the open tailgates—turn out of the dirt road and into town. *Finally.* A half dozen of the pickups swung into the diner's parking lot.

With a quick nod to Kelly, Sere slipped out the back door. If the woman suspected one of the gator hunters or his guests of being Sere's abuser, she might be even less willing to listen to the poor sap complain when his boat went missing.

~

STICKING to the shadows of the cypress trees, Sere skirted the dirt road down to the swamp. Between Joe's paramilitary training in covert reconnaissance and her upbringing in hell's swamp, Sere felt more at home in the vegetation's dark corners than in the well-lit diner.

The sound of water gently lapping at the wooden pier was like a loving lullaby welcoming her home. She hunched down behind a live oak covered in Spanish moss while she waited to be sure everyone had left for the night. Only a hoot owl high up in the tree seemed to notice her presence. To confirm she was alone, Sere tossed a rock out into the water. The only response was the owl, which flew off toward the splash.

She sat in wait for an additional five minutes. Joe's training, which had begun when Sere first entered hell at the age of seven, was so firmly ingrained that she could outsneak a black panther and was nearly as distrustful. When her heart rate and respiration indicated there was no threat—logically or instinctively detected—she crept toward the dock.

She eyed the line of johnboats like a customer inspecting the merchandise at a whorehouse. *Engine's too big—must make a lot of noise when aroused. Scrawny—I don't need some boat getting all wet on me. Nice big flat bottom with plenty of storage—you've got potential.* She bent down to inspect the last boat's motor. With a slap to the rounded housing, she proclaimed, "You'll do. Hope you're up for a rough ride tonight. It's going to be a long one."

She had the control-box access panel removed and the boat hotwired faster than a fraternity brother opening a freshman girl's shirt and snapping loose her bra. With little more than a tug of the rope, she unraveled the mooring line from the dock cleat. As she sat on the boat's railing, she gave one good kick against the dock. The boat quietly drifted out into the bayou. She hurried back to the controls while scanning the shore for any indication she'd been noticed. *So far, so good.* With the gentlest of touches to the throttle and steering wheel, she had the boat clear of the last vestige of civilization.

To avoid the sound of the outboard engine traveling across the open water and alerting the inhabitants of the raised hunting cabins, Sere steered the flat-bottomed boat into the nearest tree-lined river. The winding path out to the deep swamp would take the better part of the night. By morning, someone was sure to notice the missing boat. The hunters would be keeping a sharp eye out for her while they checked their traps, but that would be in a good ten hours. She just needed to avoid catching the attention of some fool and having him tear off through the bayou at night after her and getting his dumb ass hopelessly lost in the process. She already had hell's denizens to deal with. She didn't need to add an idiot with a gun to the list.

The farther she got from humans, the less they bothered her. Out on the water with only the night birds, water creatures, and chirping insects as her company, she was back in her adopted home and felt at ease. Moments of extreme peace had a way of allowing memories to surface like swamp gas burbling up out of calm water—and often just as noxious.

"Why, Papa?" she remembered asking. "Why did you bring me back?"

"You were never supposed to die, Serephine. The loas of the dead took you from me too soon."

Even as a seven-year-old girl, Sere had known when she was being conned. Her father never realized how transparent his lies truly were. But then, maybe it took the innocence of a child to see them clearly.

She'd looked at the soft white skin of her wrists in confusion. The self-inflicted knife wounds that had ended her life and freed her from her father weren't there. "But this isn't my body."

"Your body has been in the ground for over a hundred years, my sweet daughter. This new one won't suffer the ravages of time. You will be my first immortal. Together, we'll rule this dimension."

The old bank office where Baron Malveaux had played his evil games on the people of New Orleans was exactly as the girl remembered. "I don't understand. If we're not really among the living, where are we?"

"I've been cast into hell," he'd said, "but the fools who think they control me don't realize what they've done. I will rule this new kingdom just as I did the last. Hell must have a devil."

Sere swung the johnboat hard to the right, hoping the change in direction might also distract her from her memories. "You were a goddamned fool thinking you could steal souls from the loas of the dead. *That* is what confirmed you as the devil. If you'd just served your time and made your penance at the seven gates that Sanguine, Kendell, and their friends guarded, they would have set you free."

Sere cut the boat down to quarter throttle to avoid getting caught up in the water hyacinths. *What would have happened if you had behaved?* she silently asked her father. *Would the budding romance between you and Sanguine have helped you understand love? Would you have still let hell's only angel raise me?*

Of the people who'd helped Sere grow from a small,

scared girl in hell to the badass demon hunter, none was more important than the woman who was the least human of them all. *My guardian angel.* Tears threatened to make it hard to see the submerged obstacles.

"This is stupid. I'm being a foolish, emotional child." There was work to do and danger to face. Not for the first time, she appreciated the brilliance Sanguine had shown in convincing Joe Cazenave to participate in her education when she was young. Even though the early sessions had been over the communication link between life and the hell she had been forced into, the man had a way of making his physical training more real than that of the most ardent drill instructor. *Joe would slap me silly for allowing my thoughts to wander at a time like this.*

She focused her attention on the path ahead. The green glow she'd seen on the horizon at home hadn't come with GPS coordinates. Navigating the boat as much by instinct as by her memory of the event, she searched the stars for the familiar constellations that she'd used as road markers to the glow's location.

It still might be just a chemical-plant fire. The logical explanation, however, didn't relieve her of the nagging worry that something had followed her out of hell. And once one demon figured out the path, others were sure to follow. *And I was so damned careful.*

By dawn's first light, she'd traveled beyond all signs of human activity. She let the motor idle while she searched the shore for any hint that someone had ever ventured out this far: a fence post, an empty beer can, or even a lone nail in a tree. She shut off the motor and listened to the sounds of the swamp. *Not even a distant boat motor.* The bow of the johnboat nudged onto the shore. She hopped out with the painter in hand and tied off the craft to a young tree that bent over the water's edge. The island was much the same as every other low-lying landmass in the bayou. Vegetation so completely covered the shore that the transition from solid ground to water was hard to detect. Her foot sank six inches into the mud. The silt was rich with the smells of rotting plants, unseen animals, and memories of home. She lay on a downed tree trunk to enjoy the early-morning sun and sounds that had comforted her since Sanguine had first introduced her to swamp living.

Sleep, like food, was something Sere only partook of when it suited her purposes. What others called dreams, she knew were her connections to other dimensions. If she was going to discover what happened, she'd need to see the problem from both sides. Being so close to the hell mouth, however, made it hard to relax. "I don't even know what I'm looking for. If there is a demon out here, I'm not going to find it just tooling around in a motorboat." She closed her eyes and welcomed whatever alternate reality presented itself.

∾

SERE PULLED the hood of her black rain slicker down over her forehead. Hurricane Agnes, which had been raging for nineteen years, continued her unrelenting pummeling of the French Quarter. Only the devil Malveaux had figured out how to move time forward in hell in order to escape the storm, and with his dastardly soul finally consigned to the *deep waters*, the hell that had been created for his incarceration had returned to its natural state.

"I fucking hate this place." Water filled the street and cascaded like waterfalls into her galoshes. "You'd think with this much rain at least the water would be clean. Fucking city sewer system." She crept out of the side alley. As badly as the weather sucked, at least she was able to confront it on her own terms.

The Quarter on a Monday morning—as it was hell, it was always Monday morning—was exactly as she remembered it. The workforce, from wait staff and retail clerks all the way to CEOs and bank presidents, walked the cobblestoned sidewalks on their way to their jobs. *Must be a nice day in the land of the living*, Sere thought as she inspected their attire. Not a single person was wearing rain gear. The wind-driven walls of water soaked every doppelgänger as though some demented supreme being were acting like a nasty boy on the roof with an arsenal of water balloons. Walking the streets at a leisurely pace while hell took its toll, however, was only the beginning of the marionettes' tortures.

Sere looked up from under the vinyl hood. Not one of the window openings in the wood-and-brick restaurant across the street contained a pane of glass. Customers diligently sat at their tables as waiters struggled against the storm to deliver the trays of food. The hurricane tore through the open space like a weather bowling ball battering the human-shaped pins. From the looks of anguish on their faces, the doppelgängers must have had some level of self-awareness.

"At least y'all are still whole."

A mosquito the size of a hummingbird zoomed out of the maelstrom and landed on one of the women seated near the entrance. It lowered its hypodermic proboscis into the bare shoulder and drank its pound of blood. Though the woman continued her conversation with her companion, her eyes were glued to the demonic creature. Sere lost sight of the restaurant as a cockroach the size of a pedicab splashed water on her with its scurrying feet.

A cold chill ran up her back and made the hair on her neck stand on end under the heavy slicker. She wasn't alone. Quickly, she made an inventory of her weapons without changing her stance. *Jack shit. Wonderful.*

Creepy, cold tendril-fingers raised goose bumps on her shoulder. *Gotcha.* She reached up and grabbed the withered bony hand close to her neck, turned her body, and flung the distorted doppelgänger into the street. The momentum landed Sere in the river of sewage. As she stood up from the sludge, she shed her rainwear. Fighting in baggy plastic was a good way to end up wrapped tightly in her clothing and tossed in the river.

She could almost feel sorry for the typical doppelgänger condemned to living out whatever activity the real-person equivalent had planned for the day. The ones who'd been distorted by hell into demons, however, were like prisoners promoted to guards. They had lost whatever humanity might have been projected into them and acted on pure hatred. Violence was the only form of communication they understood. The black apparition pulled out two long blood-drenched swords from under its cape and lunged at her.

"Fucking harvester. You're not going to sell my body parts as fresh produce at the French Market." She ducked low and kicked at the bottom of his black vinyl cloak.

The demon did a somersault over her head and landed with a loud splash behind her. "Don't resist me, and I'll just take an arm or maybe one of those thin, muscular, pretty legs. You'll hardly miss it."

"No, thanks." When her opponent came at her again, Sere launched herself up toward the mangled remnant of a metal bracket that had supported a balcony and swung forward like an acrobat about to do a flip.

The demon had anticipated her move. Instead of wrapping her legs around his scrawny neck and spinning his head like a cap off a cheap bottle of beer, Sere felt his teeth sink deep into her inner thigh. His twin swords crossed like scissors slicing up her body. Instinctively, she pulled hard at the rusty metal beam, which snapped off at the brick wall. *Now I have a weapon.* She arched her body and twisted hard away from the gleaming blades. Their crash into the stream of muck drove his sharply rotted teeth deeper into her flesh, but she managed to pin one of his arms under their bodies. In his disorientation, she grabbed his free wrist, pulled hard at his spindly, desiccated arm, and by driving her heel into his shoulder socket, wrenched his arm from his body. The blade he was holding fell harmlessly at her side.

No longer in her grasp, the demon turned away from his

removed limb in her clutches and jumped to his feet. He angled his remaining weapon up from his crotch. "Was it good for you too? I was due for an arm upgrade anyway. Too bad yours are so small."

She tossed the bony arm across the water, grabbed the sword, and stood to face him. "You can add as many accessories as you like to that hooptie body of yours. They still won't give you any skills. You're like a car that's been so heavily modified it no longer drives without getting stuck in potholes."

"We'll see about that." He swung wildly at her head.

Her taunting had worked. While he focused on the sword she used to parry his attack, she pulled the rusty metal bar from behind her back and impaled him through the gut. "I'm not so easily sliced into deli meat," she said as she spun away from him and pulled the shaft out of his body.

"That's two for you." His bravado was betrayed by raspy breathing, which indicated his true condition.

"Come on, bony boy." She aimed the sword at his neck. "Make your move, and lose your head."

Harvesters never considered the cost. A fight with one was always all or nothing. Sere knew better than to take his injuries as weaknesses. Though he was down an arm and losing blood at an alarming rate from his gut, the wounds would only drive him to fight with increased ferocity. He came at her with eyes ablaze, teeth bared, and sword swinging haphazardly through the air as if he were fighting off a swarm of mosquitoes.

Defense was never Sere's position of choice. She rushed

at the demon with equal zeal. There was no safe, easy play. She slashed backhand at him with her iron bar. His sword cut her from shoulder to wrist but not before she'd landed her rusty bar into his ribs. The force of the blow, along with his blade being at her side, opened him up to the kill cut. She continued with her determined spin and slashed down with the edge of her sword against the demon's neck. His head rolled from his shoulders into the muck just before his body slumped to the ground.

Sere dropped her weapons, bent over, and put her hands on her knees for support. Blood flowed down her arm and dripped onto the demon's upturned face. "Disintegrate, you asshole." His head and body sank into the slop like meat falling off the bone into a thick roux.

From across the street, the woman who'd been weakened from the mosquito stared at Sere with wide, frightened eyes. Sere could practically hear the hellish sermon that played in the woman's mind: *This is what one gets for stepping out of the preordained path of righteousness.* Doppelgängers who showed free will and broke away from Professor Yates's projections of the real people in life either became harvesters or were sliced up for the harvesters' pleasure.

Sere brushed the gore from the decapitated harvester off the front of her slicker. "You lose, asshole." Though blood coated her arm, in hell's nightmare, so long as she won, she would heal.

She picked up the two swords as her winnings and headed toward Jackson Square. Artists never were much good at following society's ideals, and that made the area in front of Saint Louis Cathedral—with its street performers, musicians, and painters—the perfect place to find a pieced-together sentient mannequin willing to talk. She glared menacingly and pointed the swords at anyone who crossed her path.

Tourists sat on the steps of the church, looking like human remnants a gator had thrown up. A street performer mockingly danced and yelled at the spectators. Observing the entertainer's short female arms, beefcake shoulders, well-endowed breasts, child's legs, and mangled face, Sere couldn't guess its original gender. Paintings in blood hung from the square's rotting iron gates. Towering above the scene were the chained-shut wooden doors of Saint Louis Cathedral.

She ducked under the cast-iron portico of the block-long apartment building to watch the action from a shadowy doorway. "This is pointless. The hell mouth isn't in the Quarter, so being here puts me no closer to understanding where the other end of the connection is in life. If it were here, there would be a full-on demon invasion. Why would I dream up a place that's no use whatsoever?" She squeezed her eyes shut, hoping that when she opened them again, it would be to wake up from her nightmare.

The rains of hell were still howling in Sere's ears when a gutter waif stumbled into her. The girl couldn't have been much older than a teenager. "Sorry you had to wait. I didn't dare approach you after the fight in case someone was watching. The goddess Sanguine told us to keep an eye out for you. I had to be sure it was really you before making contact. Can't be too careful these days, but after seeing you willingly go up against a harvester and survive the encounter, I knew you must have been sent from the beyond. To defeat evil, a hero must embrace personal injury. That's how I knew you weren't a typical doppelgänger. What do you need?"

Sere faced away from the girl in an attempt to avoid unwanted harvester attention being paid to her companion. "Something has crossed out of hell, but I don't even know where to look. The access between our dimensions has been uncovered on this side."

"The goddess hears your plea. Help will find you. You'd better leave now." The girl turned from the shadows and disappeared back into the storm-drenched streets.

⁓

SERE WOKE up to a loud splash and a wall of water that drenched her. Even in her sleep-hazed post-nightmare state, she knew that the gator she'd grown up with in hell's swamp had arrived.

"Damn it, Lefty!" She slid off the log and shook the water out of her hair. The thirty-foot alligator took up most of the width of the river. "You could have just nudged the log or something. You know how I hate being splashed by that tail of yours."

The monster turned toward the shore and set his muzzle next to her feet like a repentant puppy. The creature's nostrils ejected swamp moisture so hard it penetrated her jeans clear up to her thighs.

"It's good to see you too." She never could stay mad at him for long. "But how many times have I told you? You can't swim out of the deep swamp toward the gator-hunting grounds. Now that the stories about you have grown beyond mere rumors, those redneck assholes won't rest until they have your hide."

The river monster nudged Sere's boot as if that was supposed to be an explanation of his actions. The show of emotion made her squat down to rub the prehistoric-looking creature's snout. "I miss her too." Sere rubbed the large scales of her boot that perfectly matched those of her reptilian companion. "At least she's always with me. I wish I could have fashioned you a memento as well, but it's not like you carry anything with you." Between her boots, saddlebags, and helmet cover, Sere had tried to utilize as much of the old gator's hide as she could reasonably keep with her.

Lefty swung his head back into the river and swam far enough out that he could edge his tail up beside Sere like a boat ramp.

"I guess there's no harm in going for a little ride. After all, I did ask for help finding whatever is out here. It'd be rude to reject the offer when it comes in the form of such a gallant gator." Sere skipped along the pointy scutes of the reptile's back the way she had as a child. When she reached the animal's massive shoulders, she lay on her back with her head between Lefty's green-and-gold eyes.

The animal's fifteen-foot-long tail made for powerful, quiet, and smooth locomotion through the calm water. The gentle rocking of his body massaged his scutes into Sere's back muscles. She stared up at the sky as he swam beneath her, just as she'd done so many days growing up in hell. The ancient hell gator that had protected Sanguine was more a pet to Sere than a guardian. *Fellow creatures from hell. No wonder I bonded with you.*

---

3

*L*efty stopped his gentle rocking and floated calmly. Water sloshed up along his bulbous body and roused Sere from her enjoyment of the early afternoon.

"You're not supposed to submerge, you silly creature. You're getting me all wet." She rolled onto her stomach to see what had disturbed her pet's swim through the bayou. Instead of the expected thick green swamp water, they were floating into a small clear-blue lake. *Hell's gate.*

"Just stay where you are. There's no reason why this has to turn ugly."

The trembling voice from the shore made Sere bolt up from Lefty's back like a surfer preparing to ride a wave. She crouched into her attack stance. Someone was watching her from the tall grass beyond the sandy beach. She slipped her hand down to her boot. *Goddamn that bartender. He still has my fucking knife.*

"Who are you? Show yourself before I sic my alligator on you."

She hunched low on Lefty's back as a thin young man stepped out of the tall grass. "Please don't. Professor Yates sent me."

"Andy? What the hell are you doing here?"

Professor Yates's teenage assistant from hell stood with his arms in front of him like a boy who'd just been caught skinny-dipping. "I'm supposed to give you this." He kicked a backpack at his feet.

Hell's swamp creatures, like Lefty, were native to the demonic realm. Sere respected those original inhabitants. Then there were the projections of real people and animals that Professor Yates had created to fill the French Quarter. As hell's guardians, Sanguine, Kendell, and their friends had needed a make-believe population to convince Baron Malveaux that he wasn't alone, but to Sere, the human puppets were little more than toys for her amusement. Not all of them, however, belonged to her. Joe had used some of the mannequins as sparring partners in his training sessions, and Kendell and the band had occupied their doubles for their personal music gigs when performing for young Sere. Professor Yates, however, took his games too far in giving the mannequins he used a degree of sentience. They didn't have souls but were endowed with a degree of self-will. These fleshy automatons gave Sere the creeps.

"You have no business on this side of the divide. Someone could have seen you. This had better be fucking important, or I'll kill your *real* just to watch you disintegrate, *Artie*."

The boy's face turned beet red. "Don't call me that. Just because my soul wasn't pulled from the dead like yours was, that doesn't mean I'm artificial. I am self-aware."

Sere sat back down on the gator's back, feeling like a guru explaining life to a fool. "Sentience without a soul results in only self-interest."

"That doesn't even make any sense. You're just trying to justify your need for the team of people who've given you life. *Queen Sere*, who thinks her servants should always bow down and be grateful for the scraps of self-determination dropped from her table."

Lefty let out a crackly roar that rippled the water and silenced Andy.

"I don't expect you to understand," Sere said. "Without that basic connection to others, you have no ability to empathize. Like all demons, all you care about is yourself. My prehistoric gator has more understanding of compassion than you do."

"And you're some great expert? Until you left hell, your entire experience with living people could be summed up in less than ten individuals, and each of them was fawning over you like you were an orphan picked up off the street."

"First I was a queen, and now I'm an orphan? Sere the orphan queen. I kind of like that." Philosophical arguments with a toy doll never got Sere anywhere productive.

"No, what you are is a psychotic bitch."

Even without her knife, Sere could list a dozen ways of decapitating the doppelgänger without even thinking about it, but Professor Yates hadn't sent Andy so that she could exercise her assassin's skills on him. "So you're the little pipsqueak that set off the green-glow hell alarm? Why go to all the trouble?"

Andy crossed his arms over his chest as if he'd done something clever and was about to be patted on the back for it. "This bag is full of shotgun shells. I made them myself under the professor's supervision."

She didn't like the sound of that. Anything made in hell would have dire consequences in life. "You're going to make me ask you *why*? It would be a lot easier if you'd learn to tell me what I want to know so I don't have to keep asking dumb questions."

He looked around as if hesitant someone might be listening in. "I wasn't the first one to set off the green glow."

Sere stroked Lefty's back like a jockey subtly directing a racehorse. *If you just took one of the kid's legs, it would probably grow back.* "You're starting to piss me off, *Artie*."

He glared at her, but instead of reacting further to her insult, he reached into the pack and pulled out a box of shells as if that was supposed to somehow pacify her. "Something else crossed over first. We don't know how or what. I'm only here because the professor rigged up a tether lifeline from hell so I could enter the gate, but this is as far as I can go. He hoped these shotgun shells would make it easier for you to deal with whatever followed you."

"So you're like a little Aquaman toy breathing through a tube." She nodded toward the bag. "How do they work?"

"Hell's creatures are reflections of this reality."

She rolled her eyes. *You maybe, but not me.* "Stop stating the obvious."

"Using a bullet created in life won't kill a

doppelgänger, only injure one of us until we can regenerate. I used rubble from the real-bank bombing projected into our dimension to fill these shells. Shoot one of us with these, and the connection to our real will be severed."

Memories of the night Joe helped Aunt Kendell and Uncle Myles blow up Baron Malveaux's office in life and free young Sere from the devil's dominance still haunted her. Even nineteen years later, she still avoided the French Quarter as if it were coated in radioactive dust.

She kicked Lefty in the side to get him to swim toward the shore. "That works if the demon is related to the professor's projections in the city. Agnes Delarosa was slightly more clever in how she filled the swamps."

Andy jumped a good six feet back from the water's edge at seeing the monster zero in on his location. "Professor Yates just wants you to be prepared."

From the water, she was able to see partway into the open bag. "And what does he expect me to do without a gun?"

"He said Joe would be able to work up a shotgun for you. Please don't let your gator eat me."

She patted the river monster's shoulder to get him to turn parallel to the shore. "How confident are you that those shells will disrupt the virtual projection?"

Andy remained well back from the shore. "It's just a theory, but Professor Yates said it'd be best if you didn't have any open wounds while you were handling the cartridges. We were a little short on time for testing. It will depend on your quarry's size, but there should be enough pellets in each shell to cut the connection of anything weighing a hundred pounds or so."

Wonderful. So demonic squirrels won't be a problem. She could tell from Andy's shaking that he wasn't telling her everything. "And what happens to the projected body?"

"Matter in life remains as matter."

Peachy. "So no disintegration as in hell?" Lefty swung his tail onshore, and Sere stepped off her companion and lifted the heavy backpack. "Professor Yates didn't by chance tell you I was to test one of these little deadly shells on you, now, did he? Or is that why you didn't bring a gun?"

Andy hid behind a nearby cypress tree trunk. "Of course not. I've been a useful assistant ever since you killed Thomas."

"That was an accident." Sere didn't mean to smile, but she could feel the muscles tugging at her cheeks.

"Bullshit. You cut off his goddamned head."

Sere felt along the edge of her boot to the empty scabbard concealed in the lining. "Weapons training can be dangerous. Joe wanted to use a mannequin that could think on its feet. Besides, Professor Yates was able to regenerate Thomas."

Andy stayed well hidden behind the tree. "But without the sentient modifications the professor had given him. He's just another mindless human copy now. I'd like to keep my personal memories, if that's all right with you."

Using her ninja training, she silently stepped along the shore. When she spoke again, it was from beside the tree in a whisper directly in Andy's ear. "Who's to say you'd regenerate if I lopped off your head on this side of the barrier?" The boy took off so fast along the shoreline that Sere wondered if his feet were even getting wet. "Don't let me catch you on this side of the barrier again! I won't just be playing next time."

She laughed at the retreating figure and turned back to Lefty. "I'm sure I'll get an earful from the professor about my treatment of the kid, but he should know better than to send that silly little lab rat."

The fact that the old inventor's lab geeks were partially responsible for her immortality only made her more mistrustful of their hidden agenda. *Sentience isn't so easily contained, my dear professor.* Lefty splashed water with his tail in the direction of the retreating youth as if agreeing with Sere.

Sere sat on the shore with the backpack at her feet. "So was Andy the one you wanted me to see? Next time you wander in from the swamp toward civilization and make me worry about your reptilian hide, find me something worth hunting."

His snort sent a mist plume that reached all the way to the trees.

"You're right. Andy said there was another. Some creature has a good head start on me. Would have helped if Andy had told me if it was swimming, flying, or walking." She pulled one of the boxes of shells out of the stuffed bag. "Based on the number of shells, Professor Yates must be expecting a full-on nutria invasion."

~

WHILE SERE CONSIDERED her next move, Lefty circled the surface of the small lake like a guardian, making sure the little demon made it back down to hell. Though she doubted Andy would be fool enough to bubble back up from the lake's depths, hell's gator being on patrol in the area at least meant the gate wasn't standing wide open for all to use.

She let out a loud whistle to call him over. "Take me back to my boat. I need to find Joe. I just hope he's not waiting for me at Big Larry's. The longer I sit here, the more of a head start that demon has on me."

Once she settled on his back, Lefty made a beeline for the johnboat Sere had borrowed. The huge animal maneuvered the interconnected waterways like a child challenged to find a specific toy in the chaos of his room.

While he swam, she pulled out one of the shotgun shells and dumped the contents into her hand. "I wonder what would happen if I swallowed one."

Lefty rocked hard to the right as if trying to make her drop the bombing-debris rocks.

"I wasn't going to do it. I was just wondering. You don't have to get all freaked out on me. Committing suicide once was enough for me." She resumed her contemplation of the miniature marbles. "I always figured Superman must have dreaded holding a kryptonite stone in his hand, but handling these deadly connections to home doesn't frighten me. It makes me nostalgic. I suppose that's the point. Remembering where I come from makes me weak. Someone without ties is free to take the path of danger."

Lefty swam along as if Sere's philosophical revelations

were nothing more than the singing of the birds in the trees. She tossed the rounded pebbles into the water and watched them sink until they were out of sight. "I should have heaved a couple of shells into the water after Andy. I'll bet that would have kept him from bothering me again."

The water began to churn where the rocks had sunk. Snakes, fish, and turtles surfaced and followed Lefty like a bayou flotilla. Sere crawled to the back of the giant gator. Animals from the swamp, like her snake companions, had always been more like friends than creepy-crawly creatures out to bite her. But they didn't typically gather in large groups at her command—at least not the ones in the living realm.

"They can't be from hell. If that many animals worked their way through the gate, the sky would have lit up like a Day-glo-green hurricane." She sat cross-legged on the tough hide and emptied another shell into her hand. Rolling the stones around in her palm, she wondered if the paranormal energy held some magical attraction for the living animals. Each rounded white-and-black-veined pebble tingled as if electrically charged.

When Sere was growing up in hell, Polly Urethane had done her best to educate her on the magical specifics of the world she inhabited. As the only student of ten instructors, Sere didn't have the luxury of falling asleep in the back of the class, though that didn't prevent her from being obstinate. Persevering despite Sere's resistance, Polly had told her, "Professor Yates's projections need hell's structures to bounce off of, like a movie shown on a big screen. Since what we're doing is three-dimensional and solid, we require considerably more than a flat white sheet. Every physical structure that Agnes Delarosa constructed with her witch spells we use to bounce our reality into your realm. The residual paranormal energy coats everything in the Quarter like moisture rolling down a cold glass of iced tea on a humid day."

Sere picked one of the pellets off her palm and tossed it into the water. The animals gave it a wide berth, but the gap they created was quickly filled with a large catfish that joined the procession. With each stone she heaved into the water like fish bait, another creature surfaced. *My personal swamp navy.*

As Sere's surrogate mother, Sanguine had offered information that was easier to remember than Polly's teacher-like ramblings: "Remember, Sere, my grandmother and I were swamp witches. These marshes, rivers, and forests and all the creatures that dwell here are more than just your home. They're here for your protection." Being a little girl living in hell came with its own rules, and what Sanguine had been prior to becoming an angel had sounded like an alternate reality—one that couldn't possibly matter.

"I stand corrected, my magical witch angel. You must have known one day I'd wander beyond hell's borders and need to rely on your bayou friends."

By the time Lefty crawled onto the shore next to the boat Sere had borrowed, the swamp creatures that had followed them had swum back to their submerged lives. She added that tidbit of information to what she knew about swamp life. *If I don't give them a mission, I can't expect them to hang around.*

She lifted the backpack to her shoulder and climbed off the gator's back. "Keep patrolling hell's gate. I don't want that little twerp swimming back here like the connection is some damn public pool and he's leaving the kiddie side for the deep end. If I need you, I'll send the snakes. Otherwise, for your own safety, please do not wander in toward the gator hunters again. I know you could snap one of their boats in half with just the flick of your tail, but those assholes can be relentless. Trust me. I know." The memory of the black Ducati and its determined rider still got on Sere's nerves. *You fucking made me blow a head gasket.*

She dumped the pack on the ground and stood on the shore while Lefty swam back toward the section of swamp free of men and their obsessions. The sun still hung too high over the horizon for her to dare her journey back to civilization. Borrowing the boat was bad enough, but getting caught with it out on the water by some overzealous gator-hunting vigilante might tax even her fighting skills.

She sat next to the backpack. While watching the afternoon fade away, she faced what she had become. When she was growing up, hell's swamp had been the one respite she could rely on. Being flown into New Orleans in Sanguine's arms meant lessons over the communication gate from Kendell and her crew, combat training with Joe, and orientation from Sanguine on what was involved in city living. Other than the physical exertion, Sere found the whole endeavor tiresome. No matter how many times the others explained that real people weren't as hollow as the doppelgängers she dealt with—and that someday she would appreciate the interpersonal skills—Sere found her animal companions far more interesting. Even enduring puberty with only sex bots to satisfy her urges came as a relief compared to joining the living and having to deal with the emotional connection that went along with the physical acts.

"People and their fucking neuroses."

The memory of her last day in hell played in her mind like a repeating song she couldn't turn off. "You don't have to go." The sunlight had filtered through the white feathers of Sanguine's wings, casting an angelic glow around the cabin. No other expression of love enveloped Sere's heart as strongly as that heavenly light.

She hadn't wanted to leave. Hell was far from being an ideal place to grow up, but Sanguine and her guardian alligators had been more of a family to Sere than anyone she had ever known, almost. On her last day, the conversation had continued to play out. "I can't shake the thought that Anthony wouldn't approve of me running away from life. The older I get, the less I can hide from who I am."

"Your brother died long ago."

Sere had paced the main room of the cabin in the tree. "You speak of death like it's some kind of parting of spirits. While you and Kendell were devoted to containing Father in this hell you govern, Anthony was the one who came back to protect me from the devil. I was just an innocent child caught in your trap."

Sere hadn't meant to be snippy. As Sanguine continued, Sere regretted making the veiled accusations. Never before had Sanguine's wings fallen so low. "You're a beautiful songbird locked in a cage, and I need to set you free. I can see that now. Your father is gone. I've been selfish keeping you in my realm for so long."

Sanguine might have come from the land of the living, but it was never really her home—just as hell wasn't really Sere's.

"I had nowhere else to go," Sere said. "You saved me, raised me, and loved me. But hiding in the swamp—whether in hell or life—isn't my destiny. It's time I become the person I predicted I'd be—the one my brother inspired me to be."

Sanguine stood a little straighter but left her wings lowered. "You're a warrior princess. That's how you saw yourself as a young girl and how you wanted to be raised, and now you're ready to fulfill that dream." The woman under the feathers had understood, even if the angel always sought to protect.

Sere heaved the backpack into the boat. "Fucking emotions." She pushed the aluminum hull off the muddy shore, jumped in, and headed back for a civilization that was far less welcoming than the swamp she loved. Like any warrior, comfort was merely an indication that she was ignoring her true sense of purpose.

Being back in the man-made boat after a day with only her swamp creatures made the hairs on the back of her neck stand on end. With each bend in the river, she stared long and hard at the shoreline, tall grasses, and shadowy tree trunks for someone who might be lying in wait for her return. As night fell, the uneasy feeling of being watched intensified. Since she hadn't spent much time around people, the gut instinct Joe often talked about always sounded more like magic than tactics to Sere. For the first time, she had a sense of what he was talking about. With only the shotgun cartridges as weapons—but no gun to discharge them and no knife—each of her muscles flexed, ready for battle.

"Where does instinct end and paranoia begin?" She spoke the question out loud as a way of imprinting a reminder to ask Joe at their next training session.

~

WELL BEFORE DAWN, Sere snuck the gator hunter's boat back into its position alongside the dock. A light she didn't remember hung over the bait station, attracting all manner of moths and flying insects. *They probably just replaced the bulb,* she thought hopefully. Any change, however, put her fighting instinct even further on edge. She looked over the side of the rickety boards at the dark water. It was either swim for it or sneak past the lit structure. The heavy pack made the decision for her. Wet ammunition seldom worked as intended, and she didn't need weapons she couldn't rely on when it came to facing a demon from hell. She kept low, hoping to stay in the shadow of the butcher bench that smelled of rotting meat. If there was a surveillance system, she didn't notice it—but that was kind of the point.

Once away from the water, she crept along the trees and vines to avoid creating any footprints on the dirt road back into town. Between hunching low and keeping silent, watching for someone following her, and avoiding every twig that might snap and announce her presence, the mile-long walk from the swamp to town took three times as long as the trip out to the water had taken the previous night. Before crossing from the comfortable shadows to the comparatively revealing streetlights, she looked down the deserted main road. *I doubt the routine in this small town ever changes. Since the gator boys can't start hunting until daylight, I should still have a few hours before things get interesting.*

The streetlights managed to clearly illuminate the signs on the fronts of the buildings but only cast an overall glow on the rest of the main road. Other than the sound of her boots on the concrete sidewalk, the town was slumbering like a high school student buried under the blankets, not wanting to start the day. Each dark window held the possibility of someone secretly watching, but with the threat now ahead of her, the creepy feeling of someone following eased off.

From the far end of town, she caught the sound of a tinny transistor radio blaring "Highway to Heaven." *I'll bet that's Larry getting an early start. It'll be good to have my wheels back.*

She didn't run into any further signs of life until she saw the bright shop lights from the open bay door of the mechanic's shop. "Anybody home?" she called out.

"Come on in. I'm in the back, trying to get some of this grease off my hands."

Standing proudly off to the side of the front door was her Triton. It sparkled in the bright work lights. "I didn't expect you to detail my ride, just fix the head gasket." She secured Andy's backpack on the gas-tank luggage rack.

"Force of habit. I hate seeing a piece of machinery not

looking its best when it leaves my shop." Larry came out of the back bathroom, still wiping his hands on a heavily stained shop towel.

Sere bent down to inspect the engine. "She looks good. How does she ride?"

"I like a woman who's not dazzled by a shiny finish. Go ahead and kick her over."

Like most old engines, the bike had a tendency to start grumpy if left for too long. Sere started her preride ritual, like a mother trying to rouse her child without causing the kid to dive deeper under the covers.

She swung her leg over the engine and gave the bike its usually unsuccessful first kick. To her surprise, the engine fired right up. "She didn't feel warm, but you must have already started her up this morning."

"Nope. I had her ready by the end of the day yesterday. I gave her a little fine-tuning after I had her back together." The proud mechanic stood beside the bike and ran his eyes over both machine and rider.

"Are you admiring me or the bike?"

His good-natured laugh was barely loud enough to be heard over the engine. "Maybe a little of both." He reached in the chest pocket of his coveralls and pulled out a receipt. "I called that number you gave me. Your bill's taken care of, but I got the impression the guy on the other end wasn't too happy about the engine failure."

She took the slip of paper and stuffed it into her jeans without checking the charge. "I'll have some explaining to do." The concerned look on Larry's face reminded her of how Kelly had assumed her injuries had been from an abusive relationship. *I'll bet she had a few choice remarks for Larry.* "Don't worry about it. Joe is more father figure and mentor than judge."

"So he's not your ex?" Larry asked.

I don't have an ex, but telling you that would only create questions I'd rather not answer. "He's the one who taught me how to take care of myself."

"Looks like he's done a fine job. Kelly won't open for another hour, but if you want, I'll bet we could talk her out of some hot coffee."

Sere was grateful for the change of topic. "I need to pick up my things from her anyway, but then I need to be on my way."

He looked down the street. "Good, because Kelly is not going to rest until she knows firsthand you're okay. If you didn't swing by, I'd have to tell her the story of how you stopped in to get your motorcycle and repeat it fifteen times. She could put the cops to shame the way she looks for inconsistencies in a repeated story."

Sere appreciated the concern from the strangers more than she'd expected. "I suppose a quick cup of coffee wouldn't hurt." She edged up onto the seat. "Climb on."

He swung his leg over the seat and gingerly put his hands on her waist. "I'm not too proud to accept the ride. Just don't do anything that would require me to make an ungentlemanly gesture."

She laughed off his insecurity and gunned the engine. "Hold on as tightly as you like. You're not going to offend me." She let loose of the clutch and gave the engine a good pull through the parking lot and onto the street without squealing the tires. *Probably best not to wake the whole town.*

Even with the added weight of a passenger on the back, the bike promptly responded to the slightest twist of the throttle. She leaned back against him to be heard over the engine. "You obviously know more about getting the most out of a motor than you let on."

He leaned in over her shoulder. "I did a little hot-rodding when I was younger. If you're ever in the market for some upgrades, you know where to find me."

Kelly stood out front of her diner with her hands on her hips as Sere swung the Triton into the parking lot. The woman's look of consternation transitioned to a big smile on seeing who was behind the handlebars. "I thought maybe Larry was taking your bike out for another joy ride. Any time he upgrades an engine, he can't help but take it for a spin—one that always seems to end in front of my diner so he can show off his handiwork."

Larry kept his head down as he got off the back of the bike and scuffed his foot against the asphalt. "Who else is there in this town who'd admire my skills as much as you?"

In spite of Kelly's original glare at Larry, Sere wondered if the two would have preferred some alone time. "I just stopped by to pick up my things."

"Don't be ridiculous, hon. The coffee's already brewed, and I'll have the griddle fired up in no time. How would a plate of eggs and grits sound—or maybe some flapjacks?"

Larry looked up and gave Kelly a toothy smile. "You know what I want."

"I swear, boy, where do you put it? I could cook you up a

stack of jacks three feet tall, and you wouldn't put on a pound."

Sere set the bike on its kickstand and shut off the petcock. "I couldn't eat that many, but a pancake or two and a cup of black coffee sure sounds good."

Larry nudged her as he headed for the front door. "Wait until you try one of Kelly's breakfasts. That woman does know how to cook."

Kelly checked the street before following Sere and Larry inside. "Well, while you were busy playing with cars in shop class, I was taking home economics."

They still teach that? Sere didn't want to sound judgmental. She followed Larry to the counter and sat next to the pots of hot coffee. "Anything new happen while I was away?" She tried to make it sound like she was just looking for a little morning gossip to go with her coffee.

Kelly filled Sere's cup. From the woman's frown and squint, Sere knew she hadn't fooled her. "Cody's boat was stolen. Not many people around here have the balls to take a man's means of making a living. Though I can't say I felt sorry for the asshole. Lord knows he's poached enough other gator hunters' lines in the past."

Larry downed his coffee in two slurps as if the steaming liquid didn't have any effect on his mouth at all. "None of those guys play fair. It'd serve Cody right if that boat was found at the bottom of the bayou. My bet is it was the Buford brothers."

Kelly poured the thick batter onto the hot griddle and called over her back, "Not every conflict originates in high school, Larry."

"Maybe not," he replied while grabbing the coffee pot to refill his cup. "But I've yet to see one of those jocks set foot in my shop."

"I'm not spending all morning dealing with your insecurities—especially not when we have a visitor." Kelly returned from the stove and freshened Sere's cup of coffee. "So tell me, hon, where did you get off to? If some dashing knight had swung into town and whisked you off on his white horse, I'd have heard about it."

Sere got the message loud and clear: *Someone's always watching.* "I found a comfortable spot to set up camp along the river." Her answer had the advantage of not being a lie.

With her spatula, Kelly lifted the first round of flapjacks and slid them onto three plates. "I hope you don't take this the wrong way, dear, but did you steal that boat? I'm only asking so I'll know how to protect you."

Larry slammed his fork down so hard onto his plate that Sere wondered how the thick porcelain hadn't chipped. "That's just rude, Kelly. Sometimes you can be awfully blunt."

Sere didn't turn away from Kelly's penetrating stare. "Technically, I borrowed the boat. It's back where it belongs. But to answer your question, yes. I did take it."

"You don't believe in lying, do you, hon?"

Sere took a mouthful of the heavily buttered pancake while she considered her answer. "I never saw much point in it. If I do something, I should have enough conviction of my action to not hide it."

Larry waved a forkful of syrup-dripping flapjack at her. "That's a good way to get yourself in a lot of trouble."

"I'm not afraid of a good fight."

Kelly leaned her hip against the counter with her cup in her hands. "And were you the one who busted up Bubba's Bar?"

"Word travels fast."

Larry pushed his empty plate toward Kelly and smiled. "Not much else to do out here but gossip. Jackson's Bluff is only ten miles down the road."

The road out front was beginning to seem awfully confining, and the first headlights of the day announced that people were starting to head out to work. *Turn right, and ride into a mob of angry bikers, or turn left into oncoming pickup trucks with loaded gun racks.*

She pushed her plate of half-eaten flapjacks aside while Kelly was refilling Larry's plate. "I should get going."

Kelly dumped Sere's remaining food, rinsed the plate, and put it and her cup in the dishwasher so only two settings were left on the counter. "Probably a good idea. I should be getting my first customers any minute now. You can sneak out the back. Your gear is in the bathroom cabinet. We'll distract anyone who might come looking for you as long as we can, but do yourself a favor, hon—don't get caught."

Larry took the renewed stack of flapjacks and pointed his empty fork back toward his shop. "When you get to the end of town, make a left away from the swamp. About fifteen miles down, you'll come on the interstate."

What makes you think I'm running? Concealing information wasn't the same as lying, and she didn't want to worry the two, who'd been so hospitable. She got up from the counter stool and put her hand on Larry's shoulder. "Thank you both. Hopefully, the next time I pass through town, it'll be a little less dramatic."

The look of worry the mechanic and cook shared was enough to convey the message: *People don't forget wrongs done to them out here.*

~

As SERE RODE to the edge of town, she spotted the turnoff toward the freeway. She didn't take it. Somewhere on the road ahead that meandered alongside the water, a denizen of hell might have pulled itself out of the swamp.

She considered what she'd heard as she leaned her Triton into the gentle curves. Bikers weren't always the best sources of information, but between traveling the backwoods of Louisiana during their free time and working outdoors during the day, the customers at Bubba's Bar would have heard of anything unusual. Stories of monsters crawling out of the swamp were hard to suppress. Lake Pontchartrain might as well have been an ocean for the amount of contact people north of the lake had with the citizens of New Orleans. Bikers out for a Saturday ride would head north along the open empty expanses of roadway, not south into the big city. And since neither Kelly nor Larry had heard of any swamp monster wandering into town, she had to conclude her prey lay to the south. She had seventy miles to go before reaching Joe's cabin—plenty of opportunities to listen in on rumors at the local watering holes or work off a little aggression.

Against the gray-blue of predawn, a cloud of rust-orange dust caught the light a mile ahead. *The only people out this far and up this early would have to be the gator hunters working their way out to the swamp.*

She swung the motorcycle into the first available parking lot to avoid the oncoming pickups. Strangers in small rural towns attracted suspicion, people gossiped, and she'd made herself a target with the bikers. It wouldn't take a leap of creativity for some hick to connect the badass biker chick asking about borrowing a boat to the missing skiff. A beat-up truck coated in months' worth of dust was parked in front of the shiplap shack. "Riley's" was written above the front door of the shack in red paint. *Bar or whorehouse?*

When it came to fighting, Sere preferred her altercations to be inside, where she could keep track of her adversaries. Any opponent would have to enter or exit the arena through well-defined doors or windows. Every chair, table, and beer bottle was a potential weapon. Counters, walls, and hanging light fixtures made for useful launching sites. Outdoors, the variables were less in her favor. When they thought they wouldn't be taking out a wall of booze with the blast, rednecks had a way of pulling their rifles out of their trucks as lustily as they might whip their dicks out of their pants and firing with the same piss-poor accuracy at any target in sight.

She pushed open the door and entered the establishment like a spider zeroing in on the center of an opponent's web. A dude in camouflage cargo shorts and a green flannel shirt lay slumped over the bar. From the smell that hit Sere ten feet away, she guessed he'd been occupying the barstool for days.

"Anyone here?" She wasn't looking for service, but discovering if Camo Boy was the only one to contend with would help her plan her inquisition.

To her surprise, the guy who'd looked to be in an alcohol-induced coma rolled onto his side against the bar. "What do you want?" he slurred.

"Information about the bayou. See anything strange crawl out of the weeds lately?"

He lifted the cell phone he'd been slumped over and showed her the screen. The bare light bulb of the dock's butcher station had perfectly illuminated her sneaking away from the boat. "Just some no-good, thieving bitch who stole my boat." He got off the bar stool and rose to a solid six feet tall, three hundred pounds.

"Easy, big boy." Sere scanned the solid linebacker-style body for some sign of weakness. She could see she had been sorely mistaken in her first impression of the man as a broken-down drunk. "I didn't steal your boat—just borrowed it. If you'll get your jockstrap out of a knot and look inside your *slip*, you'll find your toy right were you left it—up your ass."

"Girl, you've got a funny way of asking for information." He pointed toward the dust-encrusted window and her bike out front. "Maybe I'll just go outside and take those fancy saddlebags as my payment for the boat rental."

"I wouldn't recommend it." *My usual gymnastic attack isn't likely to have much of an effect on all that mass, and without my knife, I'm down to focusing on his most vulnerable anatomy.*

Unfortunately, he's probably still too drunk to notice a kick to the balls.

"Afraid I'll mess up your precious panties and bras pawing around with my smelly meat hooks?"

"Something like that." *If an attack won't work, maybe cunning will. I do still need information.*

He pushed her out of the way with one hand and slammed the door open with the other. The Triton looked like a kid's toy next to the mountain of a man as he drunkenly stumbled up to the bike. "Let's see what we've got here."

"I really wouldn't do that if I were you." She wasn't really trying to stop him, but what she'd said was the truth.

As he stuck his hand in her saddlebag, he turned to her and grinned. He reminded her of a school bully trying to steal her lunch. "Fuck!" He yanked his hand out of the gator skin bag. A two-foot-long rattlesnake had its fangs firmly implanted in Camo Boy's wrist and was twisting its body up the man's arm. "What kind of a sick bitch puts a snake in her saddlebag?"

"The kind that doesn't like her shit messed with. You might want to sit down before the venom makes you woozy."

He fell to his knees next to the bike and grabbed the snake's head. "Get this fucking thing off of me." The snake released but then resank its fangs back into the man's arm.

"He doesn't like being yanked around like that. The more you pull at him, the more holes he'll make in your arm, each time injecting you with more of his venom. He's not very old, so he's got quite a lot of vigor."

"What the fuck do you want, woman?" The mound of manly flesh was quivering like a little boy facing a session with his father's belt.

Sere opened the matching saddlebag and let the other snake coil up her arm. She then pulled the hypodermic needle of antivenom from the pocket in the top flap. She held them both up for him to see his options. "Forgiveness for borrowing your boat and a little information."

"Whatever you want, but for the love of God, get this fucking snake off my arm! I'll tell you anything you want to know."

Sere put two fingers under the jowls of the snake still digging hard into the man's forearm. Its flared head settled back, and the creature pulled out its fangs from the sunburnt flesh. Like a little puppy, the serpent snuggled his head against Sere's wrist. She lifted it off the terrified man and draped it around her neck.

Camo Boy kept his arm exposed. "Fucking give me the shot before my arm falls off!"

"You swear a lot. Information first, shot second. And if I don't like what you have to say, I've still got this other snake locked and loaded."

"Do you honestly think I'm going to lie to you now?"

She let the spent snake coil back into the saddlebag, where it could get some rest. "I'm looking for information on anything unusual that's been happening in the swamp."

"You talking about the rumors of the Pleistocene gator? Bullshit yarns spun by tour guides after spending too much time in the sun."

Sere considered directing his attention to her boots and

saddlebags, but confirming the rumors wouldn't do Lefty any good. Besides, that wasn't the monster she was after. "I'm looking for something else."

"Woman, give me the damn shot, and we can spend all day playing twenty questions. I don't know what you're talking about."

Sere took the protective sleeve off the needle. "Very well." She jabbed the point into his shoulder so hard he yelled nearly as loudly as when he'd been bit. "If I find out you've been lying to me, I will return." She depressed the plunger, releasing the antidote into his arm.

He remained sitting against her bike. "Why is this so damn important to you that you'd steal a boat and threaten a man's life?"

She looked out across the dusty road and toward the swamp. "Something's coming, Camo Boy. And all your redneck guns aren't going to do a bit of good against it."

He rubbed his shoulder. "You're not going to scare anyone with your campfire ghost stories. Me and the boys have faced some impressive creatures out there, but I haven't heard of anything recently that couldn't be explained. Every now and then, some city dude gets lost out there hunting for something to hang on his wall. A few days ago, I heard another of those idiots was spotted in the deep swamp."

Andy? That'd be too easy. "Tell me about him."

"Woman, I'm sure he's gator food by now. I can't imagine anyone surviving a night in the swamp alone, especially not someone dressed in a business suit."

She opened her hand so the snake around her arm could

lay its head on her palm and lick its tongue toward the man on the ground. "Up until two minutes ago, you couldn't image this defenseless-looking woman having deadly creatures at her beck and call. That's the problem with you rural dudes—no imagination."

Between the snake venom, fear, and alcohol, he looked ready to pass out. She pushed him away from her bike with her foot and set her pet snake back in the saddlebag. *Nothing left to learn here.*

She straddled the Triton and kicked it to life. When she reached the edge of the parking lot, a rifle bullet tore through her leg. Sere looked over her shoulder as she tried to maintain her balance on the unstable motorcycle.

A woman was standing in the doorway of Riley's with a smoking gun cradled in her arm. "I don't put up with other bitches molesting my customers," she yelled.

4

---

*S*ere twisted the Triton's handgrip as far as it would go to get clear of the crazy woman and her rifle. *Goddamn, that hurts.* She reached down to feel the hole that had been punched into her leg. Blood soaked her jeans and was filling her gator-skin boots. She flexed her toes. *At least I've still got enough of my muscles working to use the foot brake.*

She sat back upright on the motorcycle and shifted up through the gears. Tough scrapes were nothing new. She still remembered the first time she'd fought injured.

Joe had towered over young Sere—but then, at ten years old, everyone towered over her. "Get up."

"I can't. You hurt my arm." She lay on the brick-covered courtyard behind the Scratchy Dog club in hell, cradling her broken limb.

"And that affects your ability to use your legs?"

"I hate you." She meant it.

He uncrossed his arms and moved a foot closer to her. "And I love you. Now, get off your ass."

She watched every movement of his body. By approaching her and expressing his emotions, he gave her the advantage. She rolled gingerly onto her good arm. With one hard backward kick, she landed her heel against his knee, bending it completely backward. He fell with a scream and a thud but rolled over, laughing, while grabbing his dislocated leg. "Nicely done. I barely saw that one coming."

"Bullshit. You haven't let me have a free kick since I was seven. If you'd seen it coming, you would have defended against it."

He pulled hard at his calf while twisting to get the leg to lie straight. "You're getting better at reading people, Sere." Using her name was one of his highest compliments.

She'd blushed slightly at gaining a moment of respect from her mentor. "My arm still hurts, though."

"You can't always rely on me or Professor Yates to be around to heal your booboos," he'd said. "Sometimes you'll have to fight hurt."

Sere gunned the throttle as a way of distracting herself from the searing hole in her leg. "Fair enough, old man. But why the hell did you have to up the pain quotient now that I'm back among the living?"

A loud, high-performance howl responded to her engine noise like a bird calling back to its mate.

"Fuck! Outrunning that goddamned Duc again is not on my day's agenda. I'll bet anything that bitch with a gun called Bartender Smooth the moment she saw me enter her pathetic excuse for a bar."

Raw determination had gotten her out of some bad situations in the past, but her body didn't function in life the way it had in hell. The road ahead grew fuzzy. The motorcycle between her legs no longer obeyed every one of her impulses. And the Ducati was getting louder. Within five minutes, it would be on top of her.

Joe's words rang in her memory. *"There will come a time, girl, when all your skills won't mean shit. When that moment comes, find a place to hole up. Instinctively, we all understand that nothing is more dangerous than a cornered hurt animal. Let that inherent nature work for you."*

Sere turned off the narrow highway and into a patch of tall grass. She plowed through the stalks until she could no longer see the road behind her. With her good leg, she held the bike up long enough to pull off the saddlebags and tossed them back along the route she'd cut through the field. The two snakes slithered out and took up defensive positions alongside the newly formed path. With one leg no longer functional, the only way for her to get off the motorcycle was to let it fall onto its side and squeeze out from underneath it.

She lay behind the downed motorcycle and pulled her chest onto the side of the seat to watch and listen from a protective position. "I can still fight, goddamn it." But her bravado didn't pump any additional strength into her leg or blood into her veins.

The rider of the Ducati didn't even have the decency to drive past the field in a veiled attempt at not noticing her exit from the road. The loud roar of the monster ceased at the asphalt. "I'm coming in there. Don't shoot me. I come in peace."

Like you'd tell me if you were going to attack? "I don't have a gun, but that doesn't mean I'm unprotected. For your own good, don't come any closer than ten feet from me."

She listened to the slow crunching of grass under leather boots. Bartender Smooth stepped into the clearing just ahead of the leather bags. He stopped, sandwiched between the two snakes, who were coiled up and rattling their warnings. "Friends of yours?"

"They don't take kindly to me being chased. The engine's high vibration disturbs their sleep. Since they're a might bit grumpy, you probably shouldn't make any sudden movements." *Especially if they involve attacking me.*

He lifted his head and looked behind her. "That leg looks pretty bad. I've got an emergency medical kit on my bike."

"I'll be fine."

"You'll be dead if we don't get you medical attention."

"*We* don't need anything. *You* need to get back on that penis compensation of a motorcycle and ride out of here."

He eased back onto his boot heels and put his hands in his back pockets. "For your information, I prefer slow and gentle when it comes to sex, not fast and loud—though like my bike, I do have some skills when it comes to handling the curves. At least let me look at that wound."

"No fucking way. And if you think you'll just stand there until I pass out, my snakes aren't going anywhere."

He pulled her knife from the back of his jeans. "I can handle a couple of little worm-lizards."

She struggled up higher onto the gas tank. "Give me my knife back."

"Call off your snakes, and let me look at your injuries."

"Why?"

He took a slow step forward. Though the snakes increased their staccato, they remained coiled at attention without striking. "You know, offering you help is like reaching out to a hellcat. You're hurt. If you really don't trust me, I'll just call 9-1-1 and be on my way."

She aimed her fingers at the snakes. "Do that, and I will *end you*. No doctors."

"Fine. But I'm not leaving you here to die. Sorry. That's just not in my nature."

The swirling black dots in front of her eyes were forming up into dark globs like thunder clouds building on a sunny day. "You'll give me back my knife if I let you look at my wound?"

"*After* I look at your wound."

Her options where dwindling. If she passed out, it'd be difficult to get hold of Joe. "Fine." She waved her hand at the snakes, who slithered back into the comfort of her saddlebags. "Try anything funny, and those two will shoot out at you like they were fired out of a gun."

What do I still have available? The gas in the tank would make for a blinding eye attack. Three out of four useable limbs means once he's close enough, I can incapacitate him with a well-aimed blow. And the backpack full of shotgun shells would make for a good bludgeon.

He knelt down beside her leg. "Looks like Riley got you good. We're going to need to get those pants off and clean the bullet hole. I need to see if it's still in you or passed right through your leg."

"I'm not dropping my jeans for you. Hand me my knife, and I'll cut the pant leg myself."

"Relax. I don't hit on injured women. What kind of sick fucks have you been dating?"

Not all of her sex-bot encounters in hell had been with nice, wholesome doppelgängers. "I wouldn't even know where to begin."

He used the dagger to slit the seam from boot to belt. Gently, he peeled the denim away from her flesh. "That's a lot of blood. Are you sure you don't want an ambulance? Even stitching this up isn't going to get you back on that bike."

The storm clouds in front of her eyes were starting to display lightning accompanied by a roll of thunder. She reached into her bra and pulled out Joe's card. "Call this guy." As he reached for the slip of paper, she grasped his leather jacket and pulled his face down to hers. "If I see anyone other than Joe when I come to, I *will* end you. That's a promise."

"Why didn't you call him yourself?"

Sere was losing her grasp on his jacket nearly as fast as she was losing consciousness. "Cell phones don't work around me. Any wireless electronics go haywire..."

~

THE STING of a tube being shoved into Sere's leg brought her back to consciousness. "Fucking ouch!"

"Nice to see you're back with us." The sound of Joe's unconcerned voice made her settle back against the motorcycle seat. She opened her eyes and saw him leaning down over the plastic shell of a ballpoint pen, which was imbedded in her leg.

"We should leave the bullet in her." Bartender Smooth hovered over Joe like a meddlesome supervising surgeon. "It could be lodged in an artery. Removing it could cause her to bleed out."

Joe wiggled the tube inside Sere's leg until it hit the lead slug. "Normally, I'd agree with you, but this lady's anatomy isn't typical. We need to get this foreign matter out of her."

Sere was happy to leave the explanation—or lack thereof —to Joe. Bullets in bodies had a way of calling forth the loas of the dead for a quick look-see in case they were about to inherit another soul. She really didn't need those fuckers hovering around in the afterlife only to discover her body wasn't strictly human.

Joe drove the point of his knife into her thigh opposite the plastic tube that held the bullet in place. She focused on her breathing to distract herself from the field operation. *"It's only pain, girl. Nothing to cry about."* Joe's words from a decade earlier after a humiliating defeat still rang in her mind as he jabbed the knife farther into her leg.

"How is it she's not bleeding to death?" Bartender Smooth was missing his leather jacket. He bent over her, tall and muscular in his tight black jeans and sweaty white T-shirt.

Joe gave Sere a knowing smile. "I told you, Sere isn't like most people."

"So that's your name. I'm—"

"I don't give a fuck what your name is," Sere interjected between clenched teeth. *"Bartender Smooth* works fine as far as I'm concerned."

Joe shoved the plastic tube harder into her leg, forcing the bullet to follow the tip of the knife out of her flesh. "That is kind of a mouthful."

"Could we at least shorten it to Bart?"

Sere grabbed the leather jacket behind her head as Joe forced the bullet out of her leg. "Cartoon bad boy or Western outlaw?"

Bart laughed and nodded. "Maybe a little of both."

"With some military training thrown in." Joe pulled the plastic tube out of her leg and pointed the bloody shaft at the man's arm. "I noticed the lower edge of your tattoo under the shirt sleeve." Joe pulled up the sleeve of his own cotton shirt to reveal the Special Forces emblem emblazed on his bicep.

Bart dropped Sere's knife, point down, into the grass beside Joe's leg. "I would guess you're the friend who gave her that dagger."

"'Gave' nothing. She won it off me in a knife fight when she was twelve years old. Some students learn deceptively fast."

"So you're the one who taught her to fight?" Bart asked. "I've seen her moves. What was that, anyway—Krav Maga?"

Sere flexed her toes. Though there was pain in her leg, at least the mobility was coming back. "Defendu mixed with traditional gymnastics."

"Impressive." Bart pointed at the blade still stuck in the

ground. "I know a number of guys who carry Fairbairn-Sykes knives but not many who've studied the close-quarters combat system the same men developed. Mixing in a tumbling run was a nice touch."

Joe poked his fingers against the path the bullet had taken through Sere's leg. "Her education has been eclectic to say the least." He ripped the sleeve off his shirt and fastened it around the two holes in her leg.

"If you two are done discussing my attributes, do you think I can go now?" Sere flexed her knee. The leg of her jeans was nothing more than a wet rag that slapped bloodily against her skin.

Joe wiped his knife off in the grass. "I'd like to get you back to the cabin, where I can connect you to Professor Yates's equipment and regenerate that flesh."

"I was headed your way anyway," Sere said.

"Mind telling me what you two are talking about?" Bart once again had his arms crossed in his judgmental pose.

"None of your business," Sere said. "You got a look at my leg, and I got my knife back. That was the deal. You can be on your way now."

"I'm not even sure why I bothered stopping."

She glared up at him. "Why did you? And why have you been chasing me? Other than wrecking your bar, what the hell did I ever do to you?"

"You told the truth," Bart said.

"I always tell the truth. That's hardly a reason to pursue a woman like a deranged stalker."

He pointed at her boots. "You got my attention with that story about the gator. Clearly, you're on the hunt for something you don't want to talk about. I've got a sixth sense when it comes to danger. Maybe it comes from my military training. When I get the squirrelly feeling that shit's about to go south, I start looking for whose side people are on. I'm still not sure if you're about to be the cause of my problems or the solution, but either way, I'm not taking my eyes off you for long."

Joe helped Sere to her feet then lifted her Triton out of the grass. "Well, you won't have to worry about her today. She's in no shape to be dealing with any more monsters— motorized or otherwise."

5

"What the hell were you thinking?" Joe looked pissed. He stood behind his workbench with his hands on his hips in the main room of his one-bedroom cabin.

Sere sat on the bar stool and rubbed at the holes in her leg. They still smarted, but at least they weren't bleeding. "It was just a bullet."

He tossed the technology-laced ace bandage at her. "I don't give a shit about your leg. I don't even care about the bar brawl. Stealing a boat from a legitimate businessman, however, carries with it the threat of a police report. I'm just glad I was called out to tend to your wound and not to bail you out of jail. If you want to keep your identity secret, you can't create a paper trail. I thought I taught you better."

She kicked off her boot, leaned against the backrest of the chair, and put her bare leg on the workbench. The rags that had been her jeans separated to her waist like the slit of an uncomfortable dress, revealing her cotton underwear. As she wrapped the strip of rejuvenating cloth tightly around her thigh, Joe plugged the cord that dangled from the end into his archaic desktop computer. He was right. An arrest would have meant authorities checking on her identity.

Jennifer Ellen Cranston
448 South Jefferson Dr.
Metairie, LA.
Wife of Henry Charles Cranston, Attorney at Law.
Mother of William "Bobby"...

Shut up! Sere rubbed her temples, trying to drive the woman's specifics out of her brain.

"Are you listening to me?" Joe asked.

Her leg grew stronger from the electronic buzzing that regenerated her flesh from Professor Yates's original projection. "Sorry. Stealing that boat was stupid. I did, however, need to get out to the deep swamp." She lifted the heavy backpack off the floor and dropped it on Joe's workbench. "Andy crossed out of hell to give me these. Mind telling me what's going on?"

He reached into the top drawer of the battered metal desk behind him, pulled out a folder, and slid it across to her. "Have a look."

She flipped open the gray-green cover. Clipped to the inside was the picture of a smiling fifty-something-year-old dude in a suit. She scanned the pages but couldn't find anything even remotely interesting. "He's not my type."

"Right? Montgomery Fisher. CPA. Honestly, that was as far as I got before I lost interest. Professor Yates sent the information out to me."

Sere held up the folder. "I don't get it. What's the joke?"

"Last week, Mr. Fisher's doppelgänger got up from his desk and walked straight out of town."

A cold chill ran down her back. *Cody's an idiot. This can't possibly be the city slicker he said had wandered into the swamp. That story had to be an exaggeration.* She only hoped she was right in her assessment of the gator hunters' desire to embellish their gossip. "So? He wouldn't be the first to commit disintegration." Though it happened rarely, Professor Yates's projection of the real world into hell did develop glitches without any of the doppelgängers becoming sentient harvesters or their prey. The self-correcting program directed the reproduced person to self-destruct, and then a new one was created in his or her place.

"He headed out toward the swamp. Professor Yates lost track of him as he was walking along Highway 10."

Sere reopened the folder. "His real works in the Quarter?"

"Yep. He's been there for twenty years."

Shit. "So he was around during the time of the blast."

"Exactly. What do you remember?"

Though the act of terrorism that leveled the bank building—and the gates of hell that had been hidden in her father's old office—had freed Sere from her father and the loas of the dead, she had done her best to forget the night in question. "Not much. I was only seven years old at the time. Sanguine flew me out of town while you, Kendell, and Myles conducted your little act of subversion."

"You know that's not what I meant."

Do we really need to go over this again? "As I've told you a zillion times, I have no idea what goes on in the minds of those zomb—"

"We do not use the Z word here." Joe never yelled, but the intensity of his words could cut off the most impassioned debate.

"Fine. *Doppelgängers* don't have independent thoughts. We're not talking harvesters here. Those cock stealers have no interest in leaving hell. From what I saw, when a typical projection breaks free, it's like Peter Pan's shadow. It doesn't think. Without a sense of self, a doppelgänger's actions are based on purely random emotions until it dissolves into nothingness." She remembered chasing one of them as if it were a butterfly until the storm scattered it like dust. She toyed with the Velcro strap at her leg.

Joe picked up on her irritation and checked the progress bars on his computer screen. "Leave it be. We're only halfway there." He turned back to her. "I'm just trying to understand Monty's motivation. What do the doppelgängers want?"

"That's what I'm trying to tell you. They don't *want* anything. For the most part, they think they really are living the lives they're portraying. And once they step out of the spotlight of their projections, they cease to exist. The professor is brilliant, but sometimes that brain of his takes him down some improbable thought paths." She slid the folder back toward Joe. "If this guy left the Quarter, he must have dissolved into thin air. That's why the professor lost track of him. Whatever crossed out of hell is more likely to be some animal from Agnes Delarosa's original hell dimension. Sanguine never did fully understand her grandmother's creation. My guess is I'm hunting a nutria. Those damn swamp rats can survive anything. Lefty's already proven animals can make their way out of hell."

Joe leaned over the workbench and thumbed through the file. "Are you ready to tell me how you and that alligator pet of yours managed the transition?"

Joe's casual question was an attempt at getting through her defenses. Sanguine's words blared in the forefront of Sere's memories like a recorded warning. *"If you do this, you can't tell anyone how you accomplished the crossover. I'm serious, Sere. I can cover for you on this side, but if the concept of entering or escaping hell is discovered, we'll be looking at the apocalypse. Anyone you tell would be in beyond-the-grave danger from the loas."*

"You know I can't do that," Sere said. *What happened to you, my guardian angel? If it really is this doppelgänger, how did he slip past you?*

Joe continued staring at the file. "Hopefully, your prey turns out to be just a swamp critter, but it wouldn't hurt to be prepared for any adversary. Professor Yates wouldn't have sent me this information unless he was genuinely concerned. We're not talking about a normal doppelgänger. Monty didn't just work in the Quarter. At the time of the explosion, he lived in a flat on Bourbon Street. His projection was one that got torn to pieces."

Even as a young child living in the 1800s, Sere had never cared for visiting the Quarter, where her father conducted his business. Once Sere had been resurrected into Jennifer's bodily projection—and after the explosion that leveled the bank—Sanguine had told her horror stories about what might happen if she ventured into the shattered projection. The warnings ended up being the foundation of her nightmares. *Each doppelgänger in the Quarter who survived the blast is like a puzzle that has had some of its pieces exchanged with its neighbor. In your reproduction body, there's no telling what would happen to you if you crossed Canal Street. Other human puppets might steal your pretty hair or innocent eyes.*

"The blast was years ago," Sere said. "Professor Yates assured me the virtual-reality projection in the French Quarter was stabilized long ago."

"Yeah, I heard that too." Joe kept looking through the folder as if searching for an answer.

"You don't believe him?" Sere never could fully reconcile the ghost stories Sanguine told her with Professor Yates's assurances of the Quarter's safety. Her nightmares wouldn't let her.

Joe frowned and pushed the folder across the workbench as if it were a puck on an air-hockey table. "I don't know what to believe. Humans—at least as I experience them—use other people to help define our reality. But listening to you, I think it sounds like doppelgängers aren't fully self-aware beyond what's projected into them. These mixed projections might be getting a glimpse of something external to themselves. The question is, what would that show them about their true natures?"

While in hell, Sere had never given much thought to her real. The parallel girl in life was like an unloved doll that she kept locked in the closet. "What would you do if you found out you were just the mirror image of someone else?"

"I suppose I would try to disprove the idea," Joe said.

Sere looked away from the folder and massaged her leg as if it had been six months in a cast. "Now imagine that your thoughts aren't based on logic—just pure impulse."

Joe opened the backpack and pulled out one of the boxes. "If I truly believed it was my life and some imposter was filling my shoes, I'd kill the guy and take my rightful place. Is that what you feel?"

Jennifer Ellen... Sere put her palm to her forehead and pressed hard. *Shut up!* "This brain doesn't remember anything before my father put my soul in this body."

"Fine, don't tell me." He pulled a shell from the box. "But if one of your doppelgänger half brothers has wandered out of hell, you're going to have to stop him before he shows up at work in the Quarter—or at his house—and causes a ruckus. Because if he does kill his real, and the loas of the dead get wind that there's a hole between hell and life..."

"You don't have to remind me." *Those fuckers won't ever leave me alone.* She pulled matching shotgun shells from the box. Killing monsters or decapitating puppets in hell was one thing, but the line between virtual-reality game and real-life murder was growing awfully thin. "So I just wander along the edge of the swamp, looking for a monster that actually looks like a man. It might have been nice if someone had told Andy so he could have told me. If we're right about his objective, Monty Boy could have hitched a ride into New Orleans while I rode right past him. He could be killing his real as we speak."

"We're all doing the best we can," Joe said. "The professor has been busy checking every projection, trying to figure out who or what wandered out of hell. Not every creature in that dimension is his responsibility. And as you pointed out, we believed the human copies weren't capable of figuring out how to escape on their own. Professor Yates just sent me the file this morning."

If that doppelgänger learned to survive independent of his projections, someone in hell must have helped him. She continued looking at the plastic cylinder with the stone pellets inside it. "You do realize there's a difference between training me to be a psychopath and encouraging me to actually become one."

"I trained you to take care of yourself."

You only did what Sanguine asked. Is this the danger she saw with her future vision? "So what kind of a gun will I need for these cartridges?"

"I've got everything from a long-barreled single shot to a double-barreled sawed-off blaster. Though after seeing you shoot, I'd recommend four barrels. It'll look a little odd and waste a lot of ammunition, but it will give you the most coverage."

Sere had never cared much for target practice. "So what if I prefer my fighting hand-to-hand at close range instead of using a sniper rifle from some hidden blind? You were the one who trained me to fight."

"All I'm saying is, you've got shit for aim." He pulled a section of metal tubes that had been welded together off the rack above his desk.

"Fine. Considering my poor marksmanship, why didn't Professor Yates use rifle shells instead of buckshot? That way, I could load more than one round."

Joe test fitted one of the shells in the barrel tube. "Blasting a single hole through a doppelgänger won't do much good. The goal is to disrupt the carrier signal that makes his body physical. To do that, you'll need as much coverage as possible. The more pellets that mess with his energy, the better. Have you thought about where you plan on hiding the weapon?"

"In my bedroll. That way it'll be under the headlight of my bike, where I can grab it even when I'm riding."

He marked off a section of the multibarrel tubing and clamped it with a table vise. "If we get lucky and your prey is a swamp monster, you've got time to find it, but if you are hunting a human copy, you'll have to assume he is as devious as the real thing. Where do you plan on starting your search?"

She stared at the picture of the slightly pudgy jovial face. "He doesn't look like the type to be comfortable out in the swamp. If that's where he left hell, he wouldn't be staying out there any longer than necessary. I'd rather find him before he makes his way into the city."

"We have to assume that, like you, he won't be able to use a cellphone to Über a ride. He'll have to rely on other people."

But this professional prick probably wouldn't turn to the bikers I've been dealing with. "His first challenge would be getting out of the bayou. That's no easy feat for a citified businessman without a boat. Camo Boy Cody did hear of some city slicker wandering lost in the waterways, but he didn't say anything about the dude walking into town. Cody wouldn't have kept something like that a secret.

Snakebites are more persuasive at getting answers than truth serum."

"So you think fake Monty is still in the swamp?" Joe asked.

"I think he's not smart enough to have figured out how to escape hell. But assuming you and Professor Yates are right, a nice well-fatted piece of meat like this guy would be awfully tempting to an alligator." *God, I hate agreeing with that asshole gator hunter.*

Joe cut the tubing with a grinder. He scrunched up his face as if thinking through the noise and sparks. Once the excess metal hit the burn-marked wooden floor, he set the old nickel-plated tool back on the bench. "Again, we have to assume that he shares some of your attributes. Even if a gator had the balls to bite you, unless it took off your head, you'd simply regenerate whatever limb you lost—though without the professor's help, it might take some time."

"Perfect. Somewhere out in one of those bayou villages, a man half-eaten by gators is going to pull his mangled flesh out of the water. Of course, the rednecks will call in the local quack. Our good doctor will get to see the man miraculously heal. Then someone's sure to call in the sheriff, and I'll be fucked."

Joe matched up a wooden stock to the four barrels. "Rule number one..."

"Don't feel sorry for myself," Sere finished. "It's not like I was going to forget something you've been pounding into my head every day for the last nineteen years. I'm simply trying to map out the dangers."

He pointed the rapidly forming shotgun toward a wall of

shelving filled with what looked like shortwave radios. "So long as our foe doesn't get past my cabin, I'll be able to intercept any police alert meant to reach New Orleans. And if word does get past me, I have my ways of keeping the story contained." Even after a decade of being off the New Orleans police force, Joe still had his contacts. "With me keeping an eye on what's happening north of here, you could start your search in New Orleans and work your way up. If he has already snuck past us, the sooner we find out, the better."

The city gave her the willies. "I'll only head to New Orleans as a last resort." Each person she saw there had a counterpart in hell—human puppets she'd known and played with. Though the threat of the devil absconding with human souls and transplanting them into the potentially immortal doppelgängers had passed, she couldn't help seeing each person in life as having been a potential victim of her father. *Jennifer Ell...* "Stop it!"

"You okay?" Joe asked.

She yanked the cloth off her leg. "It's nothing. Just a headache from the professor's rejuvenation bandage."

He checked the computer screen. "You suck at lying, but it looks like you've received enough energy to get back on your feet."

"I'm not lying. I don't do that." Being strapped to Professor Yates's equipment intensified her connection to her real for the rejuvenation process. Somewhere between Joe's cabin and New Orleans was a woman who looked exactly like Sere—well, not exactly. The higher-class version had grown her hair long, enjoyed more meals, and dressed the part of a member of New Orleans's upper crust.

"Right." He loaded the shotgun with four shells from his desk, flipped the barrel closed, and handed it to her. "This is small enough that you can strap it to your thigh for effect or keep it hidden in your bedroll."

She turned toward the open sliding-glass door, held the four-barreled weapon with both hands at hip level, and discharged the shells into a white sheet drying over the porch railing of the fishing cabin. The small holes that peppered the cotton fabric created a rounded-corner square three feet across. "Nice."

He pulled a traditional sawed-off single-barrel shotgun from his wall of weapons and set it on the table. "Take this one along with you as well. It's thin enough to fit on your back under your riding jacket. Just leave the neck of your leathers loose so you can access the stock. I'll feel better knowing you've got a gun on you as well as the blaster on your bike."

She looked at the gun in disdain. "Single shot? Why not give me a fucking musket?"

"If you get in a scrape that you can't fight your way out of, one good shotgun blast—even if you don't hit anything—will buy you enough time to get to your bike."

"I suppose," she said without enthusiasm. Though a very similar play had gotten her out of Bubba's Bar, she hated relying on a weapon that would only provide half measures.

Joe pulled out a leather holster from under the table. "Even if you do manage to hit someone with one of these guns, neither will disable a human at any great distance, but they should give you time to escape danger. Just don't hang around long. Most of those biker dudes will be after you before your wheels leave the parking lot."

"Tell me about it." The sunset over the bayou lit up the small cabin. "It's getting late. I'd better get riding."

"For fuck's sake, Sere. Look at you. At least take a shower. There's no reason to look like an escaped female captive from a sexploitation movie. There's a bed in the other room. Even though you hardly sleep, a little catnap once in a while would do wonders for your mood."

She trusted Joe more than anyone she'd ever known, but being indoors made her skin crawl. "I know. I just prefer to be on the move."

"You're like a wild animal. Put a roof over your head, and you feel like you're in a cage. What do you want to do? Take a dip in the swamp?"

She tossed the shotgun onto the workbench and started peeling off the remnants of her jeans. "Race you to the other side of the river, old man." She bolted for the back door in only her panties and tank top.

"You are a fucking cheat and always have been." Even so, he had his overalls off and beat her to the dive from the porch, wearing only his boxer briefs.

COMPETITION WITH JOE was no laughing matter. Once challenged, the man would fight to the death. He simply knew no other way. By the time Sere surfaced in the cold river, he was halfway across and swimming hard. With her head down and arms and legs pumping against the water, she heard his loud splash of victory. "Beat ya again!"

She eased off her determined swim. "I let you win."

"Whatever." He dove under the water like an alligator sneaking up on its prey. Insulting his achievement had insured that the competition wasn't over.

Time to test that leg. She bent down hard and headed to the bottom of the river before he had a chance to get under her. Without weapons, it would be hand-to-hand underwater combat. Unlike food or sleep, Sere needed oxygen for her blood just as much as any other creature. She swung around on the muddy bottom, searching for where he would make his attack. *Fuck, I'm giving him the advantage by playing defense.* The water was flowing slowly downriver, preventing his movements from appearing as unexpected currents in otherwise calm water. *He'll be coming from upriver, swimming with the flow.* She grabbed hold of a large boulder and pulled hard against it to propel her body toward the far riverbank without disturbing the silt and giving away her position. When she made it to the reeds, she surfaced for air.

She only got one gulp in before she felt his hands grasp her ankle like a bear trap. With a quick twist and pull, he had her once again in the murky water. He didn't stop dragging her until she couldn't make out any daylight under the thick leaves that covered the surface. When he finally turned her foot loose, he grasped her by the back of her tank top and guided her to the surface. Once she felt the leathery vegetation against her head, he let her go.

To keep her on her toes, Joe seldom announced the day's

activity, leaving it her to figure out what was going on. *This isn't combat—it's stealth-attack training.* She arched her back so only her face broke the surface under the large leaves. When she rolled over, she saw his steel-gray eyes only inches away.

As he stood, the water lilies covered him, making him look like a swamp commando rising for the attack. "Not bad using that rock for propulsion, but coming up under the reeds was a mistake. Anyone on the shore would have noticed your approach as you pushed the stalks aside. Look for vegetation that covers the surface but doesn't require much in the way of underwater support."

She was out of breath from being underwater for so long. "Are we done now? I've already had a tough day."

From his determined squint, she suspected he was about to drag her back underwater for the combat she'd originally expected. "When you're at your most vulnerable, you have to anticipate an attack."

"I know. You've drilled it into me plenty of times. I'm just saying, right now while I'm on the hunt isn't the best time for furthering my education. Just once, it'd be nice to lie out on the river on a sunny day with you and not have to worry that you were going to come at me with a knife."

"Fine, we'll take a break. I just want you to answer how it is you ended up with that hole in your leg." He pushed off from the shore and lay on his back as he drifted out into the river.

The late-afternoon sun felt good on her face and chest as she floated after him in the cold water. "I was complacent. My adversary was incapacitated. I didn't count on him having a cohort who was playing the long game. Riley didn't make her attack until I was far enough away not to be a threat."

"Sometimes losing a battle or sacrificing an ally is better than a quick win."

Sere tried to play out the confrontation from Riley's perspective. "She must have seen me enter the bar from the back room. That early in the day, I clearly wasn't looking for a drink. I would guess my stance was her first warning that something wasn't right. She didn't make herself known, trusting that Camo Boy wouldn't have any problem dealing with me. When I got the better of him, she let the scene play out, watching quietly from the window to determine what weapons I had instead of coming out right away with gun blazing."

"And if she had?"

Sere had the short battle easily mapped out in her memory. "We were close to the front door. Had Riley made her move, my snakes would have taken her down."

"What else did she learn?"

Fuck! "What I was after. She waited until I'd questioned Cody before showing up with the rifle. So she knows I'm looking for a swamp monster, and she heard Cody talk about a businessman found in the swamp."

Joe's gray chest hair caught the light like cottonwood fluff on the water. "It's unlikely that our boy Monty will be stopping into Riley's for a drink on his way to killing his real, but the danger of the two meeting can't be ignored. It's her agenda that's more of a concern. The whole encounter could be completely innocent, of course."

"Like you'd ever let me turn my back on something suspicious."

"I'm just trying to get you to see the event from every angle," he said. "If you're determined to head north in pursuit of your demon, remember that he's not the only one out to get you. That's enough post-combat analysis. What's the deal with Ruggedly Good-Looking?"

"That bartender? He nearly blew my head off with a shotgun."

Joe's laugh only further infuriated Sere's sense of self-righteousness. "And what did you do to inspire such ardent desire?"

"I may have beaten the shit out of his customers."

Joe directed his drifting back toward the cabin. "Personally, I find a woman capable of knocking an asshole on his butt sexy."

"Trust me, you and that douchebag have nothing in common. Do you know he was the one responsible for blowing the head gasket on my Triton?"

"You mean *my* Triton. What was he doing driving my bike, anyway?"

"Well, he wasn't," she said. "But if he'd taken the fight as the rejection I'd intended, I wouldn't have had to outrun him."

"I see." Even though he didn't show it, she knew he was inwardly laughing at her.

⁓

AS SERE CLIMBED the wooden ladder back to the cabin, her

soaking-wet cotton panties and tank top clung to her skin like static-charged plastic wrap and were nearly as transparent. She stopped cold at the sliding-glass door. Standing at the workbench was Bartender Smooth.

"What the hell are you doing here? How did you find this place?" Though practically naked, her anger overrode any feelings of embarrassment.

Bart held up the business card she'd given him. "The address was on the back." His eyes were not on her face.

She put her hands on her hips and glared at him. "What? You didn't get a good enough look earlier? You might show a little common courtesy and turn the fuck around."

"There's not a single blemish on your body."

The stock of the shotgun was within easy reach. With one good blast from her, he'd change his assessment of her as the defenseless female. "Now that you've confirmed your lechery, turn the fuck around!"

He finally lifted his face to look her in the eyes. "A couple of hours ago, I was tending to a pretty deep bullet hole. No one heals that fast."

Joe came up behind her. "Go get changed. Your box of emergency supplies is under the bed."

She kept her eyes on Bart while she walked past him. She hissed to remind him that there were two snakes close by in her saddlebags who'd be happy to offer her their protection should he wish to continue leering. From the small bedroom, she could still hear the two men.

"So are you going to explain how she healed so fast?" Bart asked.

The work stool squeaked—presumably from Joe's wet

ass turning it. "I'm not the intruder. Why don't we start with what you're doing in my cabin?"

Sere toweled off before slipping into fresh panties, a bra, a T-shirt, and jeans. *This is the goddamned third change of clothes since I left my cabin.*

"There's been a murder, and someone's gone missing."

"So?" Sere asked as she left the privacy of the bedroom.

"According to the work order they found in his coveralls, the dead man's last job was to fix the head gasket on your Triton."

Sere's blood ran cold. Panic made her respiration instantly double. "Shit! Larry's dead?" She was ready to grab the shotguns and head north that instant.

Bart's voice lost some of its irritating bravado. "I hadn't seen carnage like that diner since I left Libya. Body parts and blood covered the floor and tables. At first, the sheriff thought it was a wild animal that wandered into town looking for food and tore the body to shreds during the night, but a witness said they saw you sneak out of the restaurant before dawn."

Sere clenched her jaw. *The sheriff might not have been as far off as he imagined.* She strapped the shotgun's leather harness around her waist and crossed it over her chest. Joe loaded both guns before handing her the single-shot. She flipped her head to the side to clear her hair out of the way and swung the weapon into its holster on her back. With the gun in position, the butt stuck up just far enough to be easily grabbed from over her shoulder.

"I stopped by Larry's shop to pick up my ride while the rest of the town was sleeping. We went over to Kelly's Diner for breakfast before I headed out. What's the story on Kelly?"

"They only found the mechanic's blood and body parts. With Kelly missing, she is a suspect, but no one believes that sweet woman would hurt anyone—more likely, the killer abducted her. The sheriff is conducting a search."

While Bart was focused on Sere, Joe snuck the gray-green folder back into the drawer of his desk. "How is it you know so much about the crime?"

"The sheriff's deputy is a distant cousin. We don't talk much except at family crawfish boils, but as it was his car in the diner's driveway, I convinced him to let me have a look. Since Riley was the one who alerted me about Sere's run-in with Cody, I thought another disturbance so close to her bar was worth checking out. It won't take long for Sheriff Newton to add up the odd occurrences over the last couple of days and come looking for Sere."

She coaxed her snakes out of her saddlebags and set them curled up on the workbench. "No doubt he'll pin it on me without doing any real investigating." The oil-soaked riding pants she pulled out were as useless as the shredded, bloody jeans. A mixture of oil and blood had splattered the leather bomber jacket that she laid next to her pants.

Joe pointed to the pile of discarded clothing. "You have a strange concept of dropping off laundry. You can use my riding jacket. At least since it isn't covered in blood, you'll be slightly less conspicuous. It's in the closet. Do me a favor —try not to destroy it."

Bart called after her as she headed back into the bedroom. "The sheriff likes things simple in his parish.

Unless Kelly turns up with an alternative story, he's going to be looking for the most suspicious stranger to have recently wandered his back roads."

She pulled the oversized jacket over the shotgun strapped to her back and checked how it looked in the mirror. Her face felt like a layer of thin ice over a moving stream. At any moment, her sorrow might crack the surface of her resilience and drown her in emotions she was ill prepared to handle. Outside of the group who'd raised her, Larry had been the first person to show her genuine compassion, and Kelly had honestly cared what happened to someone she barely knew. Now one was dead and the other not far behind. Sere couldn't shake the suspicion that somehow she was to blame. Her inner resolve returned like hardened steel being pulled from the forge. *I have to find Kelly before some hick cop puts out an APB on my ass and stops me from getting to the murderer. Then I'm going to find who did this thing and send them straight to hell, or worse.*

Through the open door, she could hear Bart talking in a low voice to Joe. "You're not going to make some pseudo-fatherly request that I keep an eye on her?" There was more testosterone flying from the two bulls in the next room than from a bachelor party in a Bourbon Street strip club.

"You don't pay much attention, do you, boy?" Joe's southern accent always came out when he was dealing with someone he didn't fully respect. "If you want anything to do with that girl, you'd better wise up. I don't worry about her safety, because I'm the one who taught her how to fight. Thinking that she needs protection would be an insult both to my training and to her abilities. Now, you wouldn't want to insult me, would you?"

"Of course not. I'm just trying to gauge the relationship between you two."

Sere peeked out from the door to see Joe's reaction. He stood, glistening wet, and faced Bart with his unflinching laser stare. His intense breathing flexed his aged but well-defined six-pack abs. "Sere decides for herself who she wants in her life. I'm not her daddy, and I'm not some geriatric lover. But if you keep thinking of her as the weaker sex who you can win over with your charms, you'd better sniff around some other filly."

"You still haven't answered how she healed so quickly," Bart said.

"And I don't intend to. Sere's secrets aren't for me to divulge."

She stepped out of the bedroom before the two men resorted to comparing dick sizes. She flipped her hair over the thick collar of Joe's riding jacket to hide the butt of the shotgun. "How do I look?"

"Like a badass father fucker," Joe said.

She smiled at the not-so-subtle jibe. "You always know how to sweet-talk a girl. Why don't you get that old BSA motorcycle out of mothballs and join me on the hunt? Might do you good to get that old blood pumping, and you could tell Auntie Kendell firsthand that I know how to take care of myself."

He stared at Bart. "Tempting, but it looks like you'll have enough company already."

"*Him?*" She pointed at Bart. "He's not going with me."

Bart threw on his riding jacket and zipped it up as if preparing for battle. "You're going to need my help."

"You're like some stray dog that doesn't know when it's not wanted. I don't need a chaperone, and I'm not in the market for a sidekick. You delivered your warning. Now, shoo. I can't have you getting in my way just because you got all googly-eyed seeing my naked body."

"Trust me, I'm not that hard up. I was simply trying to figure out how your wounds healed so fast. There are plenty of women out there I can spend my time with. Just don't go getting yourself shot again in one of the local bars, and I'll leave you alone. I don't need some snarky, skinny bitch who thinks she's God's gift to humanity."

Man, have you got that *wrong.*

He stormed out of the workroom. The sound of his Ducati's engine was quickly drowned out by the staccato of gravel pelting the wooden side of the cabin.

"I realize we never taught you how to flirt, but just so you know, that wasn't it." Joe opened his desk and handed Sere the folder on Monty. "Keep this hidden."

"Why would you think it was our doppelgänger who killed that sweet man?"

"If we're right about him wanting to kill his real and take over that life, he'd need to do it in such a way that it wasn't noticed. Any reasonable person would want a little practice before the big event. My bet is fake Monty just discovered how messy murder can be."

6

*S*ere took off from Joe's cabin and headed toward the interstate. Though she doubted Bart would have hung around after their fight, the man had an annoying habit of showing up where he wasn't wanted.

When it came to Joe, she had only been half joking when she'd invited him along on the hunt. Any speed he might have lost to age, he more than made up for in cunning. Beating her off the porch and into the river had proven that. Now that she was out on the open road, however, she embraced the loneliness that others often feared. With no one to keep track of, she was free to conduct the hunt as she saw fit.

The monotonous ride on the straight, flat interstate made for a good time to think. Though her emotions continued to boil within her like lava under a volcano's cone, her cold determination kept them in check. Without an alternate demon to consider, she focused her energy on

Montgomery Fisher's doppelgänger. *Assuming Joe is right and Larry's death was simply practice, what would fake Monty try next? He must have Kelly, and since there's no trail of blood, I'll assume she's still alive.*

Without a vehicle of his own, Monty would have a hard time transporting Kelly very far from town. Though the swamp was Sere's home, she realized most others considered the marshes, animals, and hidden islands the stuff of horror stories—a perfect place for disposing of a body. She needed to get back out on the water, and that meant a boat. *Borrowing the same boat twice has to beat finding another victim. I hope those snake bites aren't bothering you too much, Cody Boy.*

Even if Sere did find Kelly, if it turned out that fake Monty had killed Larry and abducted her, the café owner's story could easily lead to people pointing the finger at the real Montgomery Fisher, who was simply going about his humdrum life in New Orleans. "Fuck!" Sere laid into the throttle, hoping the increased speed would clear the logjam of thoughts. Kelly identifying Montgomery Fisher's doppelgänger would create too many questions. No one was going to buy that a mild-mannered New Orleans CPA went on a killing spree or that he had some mysterious double no one had ever heard of before. And even if Sere captured the doppelgänger and turned him in to save her own hide, any investigation would lead back to the real man. Finding Kelly had to be her first priority, but then what? Whatever story Kelly told that might exonerate Sere would sound like the ranting of a madwoman. *That might not be the worst result. So long as the sheriff discounts anything she says as momentary insanity, he probably won't bother reporting it.*

And what do I do if Kelly is already dead? Sere let off the gas to avoid speeding past a highway patrol car. Bart was probably right. With no one else to blame, the sheriff would make a case for Sere being the perpetrator of the killing spree. Even if she did find fake Monty, she couldn't turn him in. *I'm going to find you, fucker. Then I'm going to kill you myself. If Kelly is still alive, she'll be so traumatized that no one will believe anything she says. Then I'll disappear back into my beloved swamp. Fuck the cops. Fuck the judicial system. Fuck the loas of the dead.* "And fuck Jennifer Ellen Cranston!"

THE SUN HAD SET by the time Sere rode past the line of pickup trucks parked in front of Riley's bar. The beater from the morning was still gathering dust next to the front door. She pulled her Triton to the back of the unpainted wooden building. Riley had already proven she preferred to take matters into her own hands rather than call in the authorities when it came to Sere's stealing and customer harassment. Hopefully, the woman's brand of vigilante justice extended to suspected murderers.

Sere used her thin dagger to pop the lock on the back door. The rifle Riley had used earlier wasn't the type of weapon to be carried around as a fashion accessory. If Sere could confront the woman away from the bar, patrons, and gun, maybe she could make her listen to reason—even if it was at the point of a knife. Sere crouched behind a stack of Jack Daniel's boxes and waited.

"I'll get another case of Bud." Riley's voice cut through the bar chatter that flooded the back room behind the swinging door.

Sere waited until the bartender had just passed her before springing to her feet. With one fluid motion, she pulled Riley's greasy ponytail down hard and had the knife against her stretched throat. "I don't mean to hurt you, but I will if you don't help me."

"You're that bitch I plugged this morning. You've got a lot of damn nerve coming back here." Riley's calm but determined voice indicated that being threatened was nothing new.

"In spite of our so-far rocky relationship, I think you'll want to hear what I have to say."

The bartender held her hands out from her sides. "I doubt that, but as you've got my attention, I suppose I don't have a choice."

"I want to talk to Cody, and I'd rather not do it while we're aiming weapons at each other."

The woman let out a snarky grunt that might have been a laugh. "You know, I'd actually like to see that." She turned her neck against the knife, "Cody, come back here and give me a hand."

Sere let go of Riley's hair so she'd be free to respond to the new threat that pushed his way through the swinging door. The mountain of a man walked an unsteady line. *I'll bet you've been drinking all day.*

"Waddya want, Ri?"

Sere held the knife in the light in front of Riley to make sure Cody knew what he was dealing with. "I'm going to put this away. I just want to talk."

"You going to apologize for stealing my boat again?"

She sheathed the blade back into her boot. "I borrowed your boat, and I'm not here to debate old news."

"Not apologize again... steal my boat again." The man's slurred speech wasn't helping Sere understand what he was talking about.

"As I told you, Camo Boy, your boat is in your slip, and we dealt with our issues this morning."

Riley crossed her arms and leaned against the glass-fronted fridge. "He's asking if you're returning his boat *again*. When he went out to find it after you left, it wasn't there."

Shit! So that's how Monty abducted Kelly. In a burst of insight, Sere realized she'd been the one to bring her nemesis into town. "That fucker must have slipped into the boat while I was out investigating the swamp. I never checked the lockers. Why would I so far from civilization? *That's* how he got into town. Then that asshole must have followed me to Kelly's. I really need to listen better to Joe's explanations of human gut feelings. Your boat would have been his most obvious means of escape. How could I be so dense?"

"Girl, I don't know what the hell you're talking about," Cody said, "but you've been a pain in my ass since I met ya. And now you're interrupting my drinking."

"I know who killed Larry and kidnapped Kelly. He's using your boat to hide out in the swamp."

"You mean Runt's dead? About time someone put that little pipsqueak in the ground."

Sere rubbed the base of her head against the butt of the shotgun strapped to her back. "God, you are a piece of work. Your boat is missing, so you drink. Then I come and tell you it's back, so you drink some more. Then—when you finally head out to do some work—you find it's missing again, so you come back here to continue drinking. Have either of you even checked into town today?"

Riley and Cody looked at each other in dumb silence. Sere was beginning to wonder if either of them would be of any help at all. *At least Cody must know his way around the swamp.*

"Do you want your fucking boat back or not? Because I guarantee you, if this guy kills Kelly, he's not going to putter it back to the dock. And even if the sheriff does find your rig, it'll be impounded for evidence. So you can either sit here on your fat ass, drinking away whatever life you had, or you can give me a hand, and I can get you back fishing."

Cody took a deep breath, which, based on his straightened stance, helped sober him somewhat. "First, as my boat was stolen, I have no way to get you out on the water. And second, it's past nightfall."

"So what?" Sere asked. "The swamp doesn't fill up with monsters at night, at least no more so than during the day."

"Look, girly," Cody said. "I'm not afraid of the boogeyman, but even people who've spent their whole lives in the swamps can get lost from time to time. At least during the day, there are others out on the water if something goes wrong. Only a damned fool goes looking for trouble."

"I found my way out and back traveling at night. I could use someone who understands the waterways and would know where a person might hide a body, but if you're too afraid of the dark, I'll go alone."

Cody pulled a can of Bud out of the fridge and popped it open. "You are the craziest chick I've ever met. And that includes both of my psycho ex-wives. It'd be worth heading out just to see you get scared of something."

Riley shook her head as if she couldn't believe what she was about to say. "I've got a boat under a tarp out back. It belonged to my daddy. Honestly, I'm not even sure it floats. But any woman who wants to go hunting a serial killer at night in the swamp with a guy who's three times her size and pissed off at her is my kind of bitch."

"Perfect." Sere turned to Cody. "If your truck will start, I'll meet you out back."

"Hasn't anyone ever told you, you don't impugn a man's truck? You are going to die out there, and I'm going to laugh my head off."

Riley pulled her keys from her overly tight cutoff jeans and worked a rusted one off the ring. "I've got work to do. I'd warn you about the snakes out there, but from what Cody told me this morning, those vipers are probably your friends."

～

SERE HEADED OUT BACK, happy not to have been shot again.

Joe's teaching rang in her memory. *"If you can earn an enemy's respect, you'll have their loyalty until the next change of events. Knowing where you stand with someone, and what to watch out for in their change of demeanor, is better than relying on the blind devotion of a supposed friend."*

Cody might hate her, but he wouldn't cross her—at least not at night out in the swamp. Based on his run-in with her snakes, he'd have to conclude that every animal lurking in the dark was at her command. She didn't dare consider Riley an ally, but the woman wouldn't interfere so long as there was some entertainment value. Monty was a different story. If it was him she was hunting, which Sere was beginning to accept as highly likely, he'd proven he could be a vicious killer.

The blue plastic tarp draped over the boat was covered in mud. A pond filled with mosquito larvae nestled in the hull's depression like an aquatic feature in a mobile-home park. *This is going to be a mess.* With her knife, she cut the vines away from the tongue of the trailer. The boat's rotted painter was covered in slime, but the cable that wrapped around the winch at the front was still flexible. She unhooked the shackle and turned the crank to release a good ten feet of plastic-coated line. By climbing onto the boat's bow, she was able to reach the limb of a pine tree. She wrapped the end of the cable around the trunk above the branch and secured it with the shackle. Turning the crank of the trailer, she lifted the bow of the boat and dumped most of the water out the back. With the nose of the boat still in the air, she pulled off the tarp. The look of the salvaged boat was less than encouraging. The center thwart was rotted nearly in half, and whatever paint had covered the interior of the hull had long ago peeled away.

Cody's wreck of a truck struggled around the corner of the building like an asthmatic wandering outside for another cigarette. As he passed the boat hanging from the tree, he shook his head. "That's not a boat. It's a couple of sheets of decaying plywood held together with shards of fiberglass. I'm surprised it held together long enough for you to lift the bow off the ground."

She didn't have much more hope than he did, but she wasn't about to admit it. "So long as there's a motor connected to a flat surface that doesn't sink to the bottom of the river, I'm going."

He again shook his head and swung the truck around so that the tailgate wedged under the tongue of the trailer. "There's no point trying to drag that rusty frame on those dry-rotted tires. We'll have to load the boat into the back of my truck."

After an hour of pushing, winching, and swearing, they had the hull perched over the back end of the truck. "They make a nice pair," Sere said as she looked at the combination.

"I told you before, don't talk shit about my truck if you expect my help."

She patted the front fender. "My apologies." As she opened the passenger door, the squealing metal fell at a precarious angle to the cab. "Is it supposed to do that?"

Cody jumped out of the driver's seat. "Just get your bony ass inside. I'll take care of the door." He lifted the panel like it was a sack of groceries and shoved it back into the frame.

"If we actually make it onto the water, finding a serial killer should be a snap compared to hauling this hull out to the river."

He got back behind the wheel and threw the truck in gear. "You are a snarky-ass bitch. You know that?"

"So I've been told."

A polite person would have offered thanks for his help in the night's endeavors, but Sere decided Cody would probably see such a comment as a sign of weakness. The way he looked her over made her wonder if being alone with the brute was such a good idea.

"What?" she asked.

He turned back to the windshield and coaxed the truck into gear. "I've got my rifle, but I was just wondering what you plan on using against the murderer once you find him."

She leaned back against what was left of the vinyl bench seat and thrust her hand into the pocket of Joe's riding jacket to count the half dozen shells she'd pulled from her bag. The exposed springs groaned under the butt of her gun. "If I'm right, that rifle of yours in the back window won't do much good."

"I'll take it with me just the same. And your little venomous friends? I'm not moving another inch until I know they aren't with you."

She pulled open the sides of the jacket. "No snakes. You are, of course, free to check the saddlebags on my bike to make sure they're still standing guard if you don't believe me."

"No, thanks." He punched the accelerator to get the heap of metal moving.

"I'LL BE DAMNED—SHE FLOATS." Cody held the bow of the boat so firmly Sere suspected he was preparing to wrench in out of the river if it started gushing water.

"Never doubted it for a minute." She hopped in and headed for the outboard motor.

"I can promise you that motor is never going to start."

We'll see. Though wireless communications refused to find a signal around Sere, most mechanical machinery bowed to her desires. On the third firm tug of the rope, the two-cylinder engine fired to life. "Don't look so surprised. Everyone has to have skills with something. For me, it's engines."

"Sure as hell ain't people." He jumped on board and shoved off from the dock with the butt of his rifle. Sere held her breath as the fiberglass flexed under his weight, but only a trickle of water seeped in around the seams.

She settled in next to the antique motor. "You're the navigator. Where would you head if you wanted to kill someone without being heard and dump their body where no one would find it?"

"You make it sound like an everyday occurrence for me." In spite of his protest, he pointed toward a fork in the river. "Head north. There a couple of abandoned fishing cabins along a stretch of river that got hit hard during the last hurricane. If I was looking for a little privacy, that's where I'd head."

Sere followed Cody's directions. Instead of heading for the deep swamp as she would have expected, the waterway he indicated paralleled the road. Fishing camps sat on stilts high above the river like gigantic water bugs. *This can't be right.* If she were looking to commit murder, she'd head for the most deserted section of swamp she could find. But she hadn't brought Cody along for his good looks or shining personality. Not everyone had been raised deep in the bayou as she had. And a city slicker like Monty wouldn't see the rivers and marshes as inviting—more like good areas for getting hopelessly lost.

"Take that left bend, and kill the motor." Cody leaned forward over the bow like an overweight pit bull that thought it had retained some instinctual hunting skills.

She swung the boat to the left, straightened it up to the river, and hit the kill switch. "What do you see?"

He kept low in the boat, no easy feat for a man who filled the pointed bow from gunnel to gunnel. "There's a light in that second cabin. It belongs to a buddy of mine. No one's supposed to be up there. I also thought I heard a voice." He rose up out of his stealthy position. "Fuck. And there's my boat." He reached under him and pulled out a paddle. With two long strokes, he had the battered motorboat alongside the weathered dock. He grabbed his rifle, hopped out without bothering to tie the boat to the dock, and made a beeline for his aluminum skiff nestled in the weeds.

"What are you doing?" Sere whispered. "You're going to give us away."

"You said you'd get me to my boat, and I said I'd find you your murderer. We're square as far as I'm concerned."

"You're not going to help me save Kelly?" Sere couldn't believe Cody was just going to jump in his boat and leave.

"I'm no fool. That crazy son of a bitch already dismembered one person." Cody untied his boat, gave it a hard shove in the direction they'd come from, and jumped in before Sere could stop him. "I'll do you the favor of drifting to the end of the river before firing up my motor."

Fuck! Sere watched helplessly as Cody floated off. She jumped out of the small boat and did what she could to tie it off with the rotted painter. If Monty was holding Kelly in the cabin above her head, he'd have to be pretty unobservant not to have noticed the action on the river.

"What do you plan on doing to me?" Kelly's plea rang out across the water. Though Sere didn't doubt the woman's fear, the sudden outburst could have been a message to Sere that Monty was still oblivious to her approach. *Thank you, Kelly.*

"I'm going to kill you." The man's voice lacked the firm sincerity Sere had expected. He sounded more confused than afraid, as if he didn't fully know what he was doing.

"The way you did Larry? Because you did a piss-poor job of it. What did either of us ever do to you?"

Sere did her best to keep her weight evenly distributed on the aluminum ladder to prevent any noise announcing her approach. So long as Monty was focused on Kelly, Sere might be able to sneak up on him before things turned violent.

"This has nothing to do with you," Monty said. "Does the bug ask the shoe why it's being stomped on? I need to learn how best to decapitate a person."

Sere peeked over the edge of the deck. Through the open sliding glass door, she could see Kelly tied to a yellow-vinyl and metal kitchen chair. She was struggling against the ropes. The intense look on her face still displayed the last vestiges of fear, but anger was quickly taking hold. *Hang in there, Kelly. I'm just about in position.*

"So you're some wannabe mass murderer trying to figure out how it's done? You don't look the type—or is that heavyset-frumpy-businessman look part of the act?"

Monty stood in profile to the door and ran his finger over the edge of a meat cleaver. From the worn wooden handle and pitted blade, Sere suspected it had come from the fish-cleaning station on the dock below. "Why do you care what I do? I'd think you would be pleading for your life, not trying to figure me out."

Just like a doppelgänger—he can't think beyond his self-interest and sees attempted empathy as a weakness. Sere snuck onto the deck and worked her way behind a battered chest freezer with beer stickers plastered to its front. Reaching behind her, she slipped the shotgun out of its holster. With just the single shell loaded in the barrel and six more in her pocket, she wasn't going to get many opportunities to put Monty down.

Sere's heart rate doubled as she realized Kelly hadn't responded to Monty's latest taunt. *Shit!*

She jumped out from behind the metal icebox and held the gun at her hip. "Die, Doppelfucker!" she yelled from the back door.

To Sere's horror, Monty lifted the butcher's knife dripping with blood from the woman's neck. Kelly's eyes were unnaturally large. She didn't move, as though the slightest turn of her head might make it fall from her shoulders. The sound of air gurgling through thick blood filled the small cabin.

Sere aimed high to avoid knocking Kelly's head from her body, as if she were playing some demented arcade game. The shotgun blast didn't even disturb a hair on Monty's balding head.

"Fuck!" She quickly snapped the weapon open in desperation to reload, but she knew she'd blown her one good shot at taking out the killer.

He rushed at her with cleaver held high. *Now we're talking my kind of battle,* she thought. She dropped the gun, grabbed the top of the doorframe, and kicked her boot heel at his bloated face. As if expecting the move, Monty dove for the floor like a baseball runner stealing home base. He slipped right under her, leaped back to his feet, and continued running for the edge of the deck.

"Oh, hell no." She jumped down, retrieved her shotgun, and finished reloading the second shell. When she got to the railing, Monty had already bounded down to the dock. She tried calming her nerves to make the shot count, but every fraction of a second put him another stride away. The blast sent pellets bouncing along the wooden boards at his feet.

Without taking the time for self-recrimination, she loaded the third shell, lifted the gun to her shoulder, and took proper aim. All of Joe's attempts at training Sere to go slowly and act deliberately came flooding back. She squeezed the trigger as Monty jumped into Riley's boat.

Small red dots speckled the back of the man's blue-and-white seersucker suit. "Got you, asshole."

She opened the breach for the fourth shell. Though she'd hit him, only a couple of the pellets had struck hard enough to penetrate his suit and skin—not nearly enough to adequately disrupt his connection to the real Montgomery Fisher.

As she took aim, she heard the last gasps from the woman behind her. *Fuck!* Her shot sprinkled the water, causing a dozen catfish to surface in response to the call, but Monty was well on his way up river. "God damn it!" Sere dropped the gun and rushed over to the woman who had been so kind—one of the few truly generous strangers that Sere had met in real life. She had to lean in close to Kelly's mouth to hear her.

"He burst into the diner not five minutes after you left. Larry tried to stop him—"

"Don't talk." Sere untied the woman's hands and feet. *Neck artery severed. Nothing you can do to stop death. Make her comfortable. The loas will be coming.* "I'm sorry." For the first time in Sere's life, she truly understood what the term meant. Had she not stopped off at the diner, Larry and Kelly would still be involved in their lifelong flirtation. Now he was dead, and Kelly was about to join him. Sere had never felt a stronger feeling of self-loathing. "I have to go." She caressed the dying woman's hair from her face. The light was quietly fading from Kelly's eyes as tears filled Sere's.

She turned and rushed back to the porch railing. "God fucking dammit!" The words rushed out of her mouth in one long scream across the water. She couldn't bear to turn around. Though Sere wasn't afraid of death, she had no idea how long she'd have before the loas turned up to claim the woman's soul. *Would they even notice me?* It wasn't a chance Sere could risk.

She slid down the ladder and ran to the fish-cleaning station below the porch. Under the sink, she found a box of large black trash bags. With no available boat in sight, she'd have to swim for it, but she wasn't about to abandon her clothing for the sheriff to use as one more nail in her coffin. She stripped down completely and pulled one shotgun shell from her jacket before stuffing everything in the doubled-up plastic bags. With a six-foot length of rope, she tied the bag to her waist.

"This has been a tough couple of days." She tossed the shotgun shell into the water without bothering to crack it open and dove into the river. A snapping turtle the size of a manhole cover drifted up under her. Grabbing hold of its shell, she directed it toward Monty in the rapidly disappearing motorboat.

7

*S*ere pulled hard against the turtle's shell to get her head above water. Surfacing reconnected Sere to her surroundings. The moment wasn't just to satisfy her need to breathe. Fresh air was like a slap in the face to snap her out of her thoughts, but the cool night breeze—and the mental break it provided—lasted only a moment. As she lowered her head back behind the animal's shell, memories of Kelly's ordeal returned.

Sere had never seen someone die before. The event shook her. For nearly all of her life, the doppelgängers she'd lived with were little more than dolls without emotions. Even if one got hurt, it could regenerate any missing parts like a lizard whose tail got cut off, and if one died, it could easily be replaced. Kelly had been mortally wounded, and there hadn't been a damn thing Sere could do to help—no magical bandage, no spiritual connection, nothing. She'd just stood there like a goddamned idiot. Even if Sere hadn't seen the woman's emotions displayed in her eyes, her feelings had worked like an energy tsunami that swept Sere up in its intensity. Like a swimmer doing the breaststroke, Sere lunged back to the surface for another cleansing breath of air before returning to her living nightmare of death.

Right at that moment, Kelly's soul was somewhere in Guinee, trying to explain her life to paranormal beings who thought they had some divine authority over humanity. *Godforsaken assholes, more like it.* Sere's own time with the loas had been mercifully short. Children seldom were forced to stay in purgatory for more than a day.

Why couldn't Kendell have found someone else to watch over the devil? Even as a child, Sere had known the answer. Baron Malveaux had only shown complete and selfless love to one person: his daughter Serephine. Kendell needed the most powerful soul she could find to contain what Malveaux had become, and that was young Sere. What none of the gate guardians could have known was that the devil would pull young Sere out of Guinee and into his hell.

Fuck, this isn't about me. She twisted the turtle's shell toward the surface so she could stay above the water long enough to get a look at where they were headed. Hopefully, the animal was following the vibrations from the outboard motor, but it could just as easily be looking to Sere for navigation. In the moonlight, tree limbs draped with Spanish moss cast shadows on the winding river.

"I have no idea where we are or where that asshole motored off to." She looked down at the round shell. "If you can hear me, head toward civilization."

Once back fully underwater, the turtle banked to the

right while Sere continued her contemplations. *That's the difference between me and Monty. Though I could easily turn the murder into being about me, I feel the connection to Kelly. He never would.* Kelly would find peace with the loas—of that, Sere had no doubt. Whatever minor harm Kelly and Larry might have caused in their lives, no one could fake the inherent decency they'd both shown Sere. Their deaths were true tragedies. Some might have said the same about Serephine Malveaux—the young daughter of the city's most powerful banker who took her own life—but the loas took a dim view of people who cut their time short. And Sere's life had been very short indeed. *Rest easy, my friends. I hope you two share in the love you couldn't quite find in life.*

〜

BY DAYBREAK, Sere had spotted the first hunting cabin. Though Riley's boat was nowhere to be seen, she needed to get out of the river and start a more traditional hunt. She patted the thick shell as her goodbye and let go of the turtle to start her swim toward the dock. On reaching the foot of the aluminum swimming ladder, she wrapped in her hand the rope to the plastic bag filled with her belongings and climbed up to the deck that surrounded the cabin.

"We need to stop meeting like this."

Bartender Smooth's voice had her instinctively covering her body. "You have got to be fucking kidding me."

He set aside his fishing pole. "So you're a swamp mermaid. That explains a lot, like how you leave the water magically healed. You haven't needed another swim after getting shot again, have you?"

"Would you please, for once, be a gentleman and get me a towel?"

He got up and pulled the beach towel from the back of his chair. "I'm sorry. I thought as a mermaid you might prefer to be wet and naked."

She snatched the terrycloth from his hands. "I'm not a fucking mermaid." *I'm a creature from hell. Yeah, that should make for a more believable explanation.* She wrapped the towel around her body and bent down to grab her bag.

He stood with his arms folded. "Well, I can't wait to hear your explanation for this situation."

She opened the bag and pulled out her clothing, which she slid on under the towel. "What makes you think I owe you one?"

"This is my cabin. Since you were headed out to clear your name the last time I saw you, I'm guessing you're still in trouble with the law. I wouldn't want to be charged with being an accessory after the crime."

Once again dressed, she regained some semblance of composure. The shotgun didn't hurt either. She made a show of swinging it into the holster behind her back. "Fine. But you asked for it. I found Larry's murderer, and I was there when he slit Kelly's throat. She's lying dead on the floor of some abandoned hunting cabin a few miles downstream."

His snarky arrogance mellowed to something resembling caring. "That must have been horrible."

"I've seen worse. The murderer headed this way in a

broken-down skiff. Did you happened to see anything like that while you were out here jerking your morning rod?"

"Nice," he responded to her jab. "If he'd have come puttering this way, I'd have heard him."

She looked around the bayou. "There must be a hundred waterways out here he could have taken. Damn it! I had one good shot at that asshole, and I missed."

Bart looked her over then peered over the edge of the dock. "So what's your plan now? Gonna hunt him down on foot now that you couldn't outswim him?"

Shit. "I need to get back to my motorcycle. It's behind Riley's bar. Mind giving me a lift?" Asking Bart for help stuck in her throat like swallowing an angry crawfish.

"Wow. Did you hurt yourself just now? Asking me for help is something new." He hitched up his jeans as if he'd just scored a conquest. "I feel like we're making some progress in our relationship."

"Toward what? I need a ride twenty miles down the road. It's not like I agreed to give you a blowjob as payment."

"Maybe not," he said, "but you are the one who keeps showing up without her clothes on and making all the sexual innuendoes."

"I don't see what that has to do with anything. You're the one who keeps following me like some creeper."

He waved at the dock. "This is my house. You're the one who climbed up here naked. I really can't see how that's my fault."

She was desperate to change the subject away from her repeated embarrassments. "Can we please just go? I've got a murderer to catch and a sheriff to keep off my tail." Not to mention the loas of the dead, who were probably all too interested in hearing how Kelly had died and who had been present at the time.

He led the way up the dirt path to the garage beside the cabin. Once he opened the overhead door, she stood face-to-face with his Ducati Monster. *I've ridden on the backs of alligators. I can certainly ride on you.* As he got on the beast and fired it up, she realized it wasn't the bike that intimidated her—it was the prospect of riding on the back. He pulled the motorcycle out into the light and motioned for her to climb on. *You could at least make it look like you were scooching that muscular ass of yours up to make room for me.* She'd had too much of him making her feel self-conscious to ask for the additional space.

Climbing onto the elevated back end, she pressed her feet to the passenger pegs and forced her crotch tightly against the top of his rock-hard glutes. She grabbed him around the waist and ground her body aggressively against his. "Make it fast."

Bart released the clutch and hit the throttle so hard Sere had to lean her chest down onto his back to maintain her balance. *So this is how it's going to be. Fat chance, bucko.* Once she regained her composure, she bent her head over his shoulder to anticipate the road ahead. Like any good horse trainer, she needed to see what he could do before showing him who was really in charge. His mastery of the motorcycle through town was pedantic at best, but then, he probably didn't want to show up his Harley-loving patrons, who were probably all still groggy from their hangovers. *I guess I should be grateful he isn't advertising my presence.*

But being the sweet, submissive girl on the back of some big muscular guy's crotch rocket was never Sere's style. As soon as he hit the gentle bend out of town, she swung her hips hard to the side of his, forcing the bike from the mild angle into a far more aggressive cut through the turn. Bart had to hit the gas to keep the bike steady.

"Do you mind if I do the driving?" he yelled over his shoulder.

"A little bit, yeah." She hooked her fingers into the belt loops of his tight jeans and yanked his butt hard upright while shifting her hips farther onto the seat. "This bike didn't seem to be slow while you were chasing me. What's the deal? Can't perform when someone else is on board? I always figured these crotch rockets weren't much more than masturbatory aids."

"Shut up and hang on." He ran through the gears so fast that she wondered if he ever fully released the clutch handle. The lazy pastoral highway became a high-speed slalom course. But no matter how hard Bart took the curves, Sere leaned her knee even farther toward the blurring white lines on the pavement below.

When Kelly's Diner came into view, Sere turned her face away, but the image of police cars, yellow warning tape, and men in uniforms had been instantly and indelibly imprinted on her mind. Bart hit the brakes, causing her crotch to ride up under his jacket and against his bare back.

She clamped her arms and thighs around him. "Get me out of here. If the cops see me, I'm toast."

"That's why I slowed down. My cousin on the force will assume I'm just scaring some innocent young thing to get her to swoon over me. So long as he thinks I'm flirting, he'll tell his buddies I'm not a problem. Had I punched it, he might have come after me with sirens blaring."

That made sense, but she didn't want to give him the satisfaction of acknowledging his consideration for her safety. "Think you can find a way around Larry's machine shop?"

He patted her on the leg as she settled back onto the seat. "No problem."

She kept her hands on his hips as he guided the powerful bike through the city streets, but she refrained from taking the lead again. Each house they passed could have been Kelly's or Larry's—each person a friend or relative. People in small towns stuck together, and she was responsible for the community losing two of its best. She buried her face in the back of Bart's leather jacket in shame. *I'll never show my face in this town again.* For the rest of the ride, she let his hips direct the action.

When they entered Riley's parking lot, she edged toward the back of the seat. "You can drop me off here."

He stopped the motorcycle and stood upright with his hands on his hips like a virgin who'd just been given it hard, doggy style. "I thought your bike was parked out back."

That's what she said. Sere smiled at her private joke. "It is. I've got something I need to attend to first." She hopped off the rear of the Ducati with a new appreciation for the bike's hard, vibrating ride. As she walked up to Cody's truck, she pulled out her knife. With quick, penetrating blows, she slashed all four of his tires. Each time she thrust her blade into the thick rubber, she envisioned the sharp tip plunging into the fat asshole's gut. "If you'd just hung around, maybe Kelly would still be alive," she grumbled.

"I almost hate to ask, but do you want me to come with you, or was this just a wham bam thank you ma'am?"

She slipped the blade back into her boot with a feeling of sexual release. "Don't you have some drinks to mix or bottles to pop open?"

"It's eight in the morning. Even my regulars don't show up until ten."

Sere wasn't sure what transportation Monty would find, but she was positive of his destination. "I'm headed down to New Orleans. I won't be back this way for a few days at least. Do what you can to keep the sheriff off my ass, but don't go getting yourself in trouble. Tell him about Kelly. I can't stand the idea of that poor woman's body left out there for the vultures."

"How am I supposed to explain what I know about her location without mentioning you?"

"You're clever. I'm sure you'll come up with something."

He sat back on the bike and scrunched his butt into its familiar location on the seat. "That may be the first semicompliment you've given me."

She gave him a seductive smile before heading for the back of the building. "Consider it my thanks for the ride."

THE HUMID AIR that rose from the swamp and battered

Sere's face as she raced down the highway tasted like fresh gumbo, rich with the smells of mysterious spices and seafood. She swung the motorcycle from side to side like a dance partner, happy to no longer be dependent on others for her transportation. Now that she once again had time alone to think, she hoped to make sense of the rush of people who'd been streaming into her life lately.

Larry and Kelly had been kind, generous, decent people. And they were dead because they'd met Sere. The couple would forever be a reminder of her responsibility to protect the living from the demons that had followed her out of hell.

Cody and Riley were assholes who only looked out for themselves, and they'd weathered meeting Sere with little more than a few days' worth of irritations. Not everyone in this strange realm was worthy of Sere's protection or in need of it. Identifying the difference, however, had to be more involved than separating out those who had been nice to her from those who had pulled out a gun.

Bart needed his own category. For Sere, sexual desire while living in hell had been easily satisfied with any doppelgänger she found attractive at the time. Like looking at porn, she simply focused on whatever her libido took a fancy to and bent the puppet to her desires. Bart, however, wasn't some mindless drone for her to have her way with. He had his own longings. Dealing with him versus the sex bots was comparable to playing poker instead of solitaire. And she only enjoyed competition when she knew she could win. *If I keep up this flirtation, one of us is going to get hurt or killed. Why the hell are people so damn confusing?*

The threat focused her back on Monty. She straightened the bike and laid into the throttle so hard the front tire momentarily came off the pavement. His first two murders were effective but messy. If he expected to take over Montgomery Fisher's life after killing him, the murder would need to be much more elegant and leave no possibility of someone finding the body. A hundred miles stood between Jackson's Bluff and New Orleans—with plenty of small hamlets in between for Monty to refine his technique in seclusion. Chasing after him would only put Sere at the scene of each crime, and she already had one sheriff who had his sights on her as the most likely psychopath. Others, like Larry and Kelly, would die. There wasn't much she could do about that. Saving them wasn't her job. Killing the demon from hell was. *And if I fail?* It wasn't a question she could contemplate while speeding her way to New Orleans.

Focus on your desired result, not on the failure you fear. Joe made an art form of boiling down a complex idea into a simple sentence. Fake Monty had no soul. That made *killing* him the wrong term. She wasn't *killing* anyone because he wasn't human, or even animal, for that matter. Creatures working on pure instinct, however, could be notoriously hard to find and destroy. Without a consciousness to appeal to, Monty would kill to watch the effect it would have on Sere—just as he'd done with Kelly.

There was another, far more ominous solution, one that would cross the line from defender of humanity to self-appointed executioner. Monty might be impossible to stop before he killed again, but Mr. Fisher, CPA and member of New Orleans business community, would be a sitting duck.

"I'm not murdering Montgomery Fisher." Saying the idea out loud worked like a sign post to turn her destructive thoughts to a more productive direction. Having watched Kelly die, the idea of killing Monty's real to see if it would make the serial killer disintegrate was no longer an option. "I'm not a killer—I'm an exterminator. I have to end Monty and save his real. There's no other way to keep the loas out of my business." Besides, if she and Joe were correct, the doppelgänger believed killing Mr. Fisher would clear the way for Monty to take his place. There was just no way to know how life worked on demons from hell. Doing Monty's dirty work could create exactly what she was trying to prevent.

But it wasn't just her soul's fate that was at risk. Monty might be the problem standing front and center, but somewhere in hell were answers to the much bigger questions of how he'd become sentient, who'd helped him escape, and what nightmare that entity intended to unleash among the living.

"One thing at a time, girl. Monty has already seen me, so I'll need a disguise."

~

WELL BEFORE HITTING the suburbs of New Orleans, she swung the Triton onto an off-ramp lined with shabby strip malls. The danger and—she had to admit it—the allure of continuing a few more miles to the middle-class mall and risking running into Jennifer Cranston was too strong to ignore. Sere's fashion-conscious real, however, wouldn't be caught dead in the '60s-era buildings that housed businesses catering to women who wanted a throwaway persona. Sere pulled into the parking lot filled with twenty-year-old beater sedans. Looking through the windows at the empty fast-food containers and blankets that filled the back seats, she wondered how many of the cars qualified as primary residences. Based on the condom wrappers on the floors, some of them could well have doubled as places of employment.

She hit the buzzer to Harry's House of Wigs and waited for the cashier to push the corresponding button unlocking the security steel-bar door. The gate popped open as if the hinges had been bent out of place by an abusive client. "How can I help you, sweetie?"

Sere ran her fingers through her short, thin, helmet-flattened locks. "I need something to cover this red hair. I stand out like a carrot in a produce bin of yellow and brown potatoes. Nothing too expensive, but something that will help me blend in without looking like I'm hiding."

"Gotcha. So no neon-purple with glitter tips." The woman walked out from behind the counter and looked over Sere's face. "Brunette is usually best for passing unobserved, but if we go too dark, your light eyebrows and complexion are going to be a tip-offs that the do is fake."

Sere thought back to the image of her real that had haunted her during her leg's reconstruction. Jennifer had long hair that she struggled to infuse with body. She also dyed it as light as she could while maintaining a hint of red.

Fucking vain woman. Sere needed to be as far from recognizable as possible to anyone Jennifer might know. "I'll wear dark glasses."

The shop attendant nodded knowingly. "I've got a shoulder-length black number with bangs. It's straight like your natural hair. That's about the best I can do on a budget. The previous owner had to get out of town in a hurry, so you might not want to be seen around Kenner wearing it." She took the ratty-looking wig off a white Styrofoam head.

Sounds like I'll be trading one dangerous persona for another. Sere held up the fake hair, wondering when it had last been cleaned. She pulled it over her head and fluffed up the black locks. The shop attendant handed Sere a mirror. *I look ridiculous.*

"Not bad." The saleswoman took a pair of oversized dark glasses from a rotating display next to the counter and slipped them on Sere's face. "Not bad at all. Add a change of clothing, and no one will recognize you."

"At least not anyone I know."

"Isn't that the point?" The woman headed back for the register without waiting for a reply. "Cash or charge?"

Sere pulled out the twenties Kelly had given her. *Looks like you were more right than you knew about me needing this money.*

The cashier gave Sere a knowing smile. "There's a discount for cash. Most of my clients like to stay anonymous. If you take the next freeway off-ramp, you'll run into an outlet mall. They have a couple of reasonably priced clothing stores."

Sere stashed the change in her jeans. "Thanks for everything."

Once outside, Sere caught sight of her reflection in the shop window. The sales girl was right. In her jeans, leather coat, and alligator boots, her hair color didn't make much of a difference. Monty would spot her a mile away. With Sere straddling her Triton, the attempted disguise of wig and glasses was laughable.

"Okay. One thing at a time. It's not like Monty is barreling down on me. A change of clothing shouldn't be that hard."

The wig under her helmet made for awkward riding. With each change in wind direction, the layers of protection slid around, forcing her to slow down and readjust her skullcap. She gratefully took the next off-ramp and parked her motorcycle among the throngs of SUVs and family sedans. The interconnected concrete boxes a city-block long didn't have a single window.

"What a god-awful-looking place." She got off her bike and set her helmet on her saddlebags. Her wig needed to be rotated a quarter turn to sit correctly on her head. "The snakes should be glad I'm not hauling them around with me, though lord knows I could use the emotional support."

The rattling from against the inside of the leather saddlebags was all the answer Sere needed. Large air-conditioned concrete cities were no place for swamp creatures, be they reptilian or human. Walking across the field of hard black asphalt hurt her feet. Boots were meant for use on grass and soft dirt, not imitation solid rock. The wig and glasses made her self-conscious. Monty wouldn't be anywhere close to the mall, and the odds of running into Jennifer were pretty remote, but Sere needed to get used to the disguise.

The wall of glass separated as she approached the entrance, like the gates of hell welcoming in another of the damned. The difference, of course, was that Sere didn't have any fear of hell—a mall full of possession-hungry people, however, gave her the shakes. Empty-handed people rushed passed her like lemmings, while those with arms full of boxes and bags struggled against the flow.

Sere stood on the marble floor and gazed at the towering concrete-and-glass storefronts. She shivered as much from the cold air as the emotional cesspool of advertisements. With her head down, she walked into the modern-day cave with her hands thrust into Joe's jacket. *God, I wish you were here with me.*

"We have continuing coverage of the swamp strangler." Sere stopped cold at the entrance of the bar. On the TV, a female reporter—probably chosen because of her large breasts and sympathetic smile—was attempting to look like a professional with the story of the century. "So far, we have the confirmed killing of four people: a man and woman brutally dismembered outside of Jackson's Bluff, a motorist who had the misfortune to suffer a tire blowout and endured a dozen knife wounds from her supposed good Samaritan, and most recently, a convenience-store clerk. No word yet on how he was killed."

Sere squinted with hatred at the reporter. *Too bad for you, you sick fuck. Even from this side of the TV screen, I can tell you're getting off on reporting the carnage.* Two pencil drawings appeared behind the reporter. "This just in." The woman's voice rose so fast Sere wondered if some production assistant had just stuck his hand up the bimbo's skirt under the desk. "Police are looking for any information on these two individuals." Sere listened to the descriptions in stunned panic. The drawings were crude but accurate.

"Look at that, Jenny. That drawing could be of you."

Sere didn't dare turn toward the women behind her.

"Right. Like I'd ever do that to my hair. And when was the last time I weighed a hundred pounds?"

There was an expectant moment of silence behind Sere, then both women answered at once as if reading each other's minds. "Junior-year cheerleading camp!"

Oh my God, please leave. Sere dropped her attention from the TV to the reflection in the floor-to-ceiling bar window. Behind her, a woman with long, straight strawberry-blond hair that curled slightly at the ends was laughing and clutching her friend as if they'd just shared the funniest joke ever told. *Suddenly, I understand the doppelgängers' desire to kill their reals. This woman simply cannot be Jennifer Ellen Cranston.* But as Sere consulted their shared memories, she knew the airhead was none other than the human who'd supplied Sere with her body's blueprint. The longer she focused on their connection, the less in touch Sere became with her body. *No!*

"Are you okay, Jenny?" The friend's voice sounded both beside and behind Sere as if she were listening to too many stereo speakers.

"Sorry, I just got a little light-headed. That last mimosa might have been a mistake."

"As if," her companion said, laughing.

Sere ducked away from the women and headed the direction they'd come from. As she hurried down the promenade lined with shops, the woman's memories continued to play for Sere like a bad Lifetime Channel movie—a form of entertainment Jennifer apparently enjoyed way too much. *How did I ever survive your high school years? Next time I see Professor Yates, I need to thank him for filtering out all that girl's drivel. How could you have been that obsessed with boys? Honestly, one cock looks pretty much like the next.*

She put her hands to her temples and forced her memories of living in the swamp back to front and center. "As soon as I kill Monty, I'm returning to the swamp and never leaving," she said so quietly no one would hear. She kept facing forward in the fear that Jennifer and her cheerleading-bitch friend might have forgotten which way to turn and ended up following her. *They'd be just dumb enough to retrace their steps and still marvel at the stores they'd just left. No wonder people spend hours in this place. They're too stupid to figure out how to get out, just like rats in a maze being rewarded with cheese at every turn.*

At Village Vintage Attire, Sere finally found the nerve to look behind her. Like ditching a kid sister—something Jennifer had made into an art form—Sere discreetly searched the crowd to make sure she hadn't been followed.

"I'm digging the whole *Daddy was a biker* vibe. The boots

are a bit over the top, though. What new look are you going for today?"

Sere turned away from the cavernous mall to face the saleswoman standing next to the entrance. Her long, flowing blond hair made a smooth transition to the billowy hippie-style dress. Sere wondered if telling the woman about the shotgun strapped to her back would make the fake hippie reconsider her opinion about the daddy issues. From behind the counter, the same reporter was blaring from the cashier's laptop, updating the latest information on the serial killer. Sere adjusted her sunglasses to hide as much of her face as possible. "The news today is just awful."

The saleswoman turned toward the back of the store. "Emily, would you please turn that off."

Sere suppressed a smile at seeing her ploy work so well. *News stories about serial killers aren't exactly conducive to shopping for frilly garments, I suppose. Gotta keep the money flowing.* No longer seeing her likeness broadcast on the monitor, Sere turned back to the store manager. "I'm having dinner with my aunt and uncle. They're not fans of my motorcycling adventures. I need something that won't offend them but also won't drain every penny I have." Again, it wasn't a lie. If she went down to New Orleans and didn't see Kendell and Myles, Joe might develop a new form of martial arts just to whip her ass.

"We have some lovely vintage cotton dresses." The woman put her hands on Sere's waist and drew in the leather jacket. "With your cute little figure, a yellow-and-white polka-dotted sundress with a wide white-leather belt would be simply scrumptious. And maybe some vintage Keds sneakers?"

You seriously have to be fucking kidding me. Sere tried not to vomit at the image of her as a good, sweet little girl. "Sounds perfect." *I swear to God, Joe, if you only knew what I have to go through just so you don't have make up a lame excuse to Myles and Kendell.* But the change of clothing wasn't just about seeing the couple who'd done so much to save her soul. In her black hair, sunglasses, and feminine dress, Sere could walk right up to Monty and stab him between the ribs without him ever realizing her true identity. And she still had to contend with the newscasts displaying her image to the brain-dead masses hungry for a little titillation. *It's just a temporary change of clothing.*

The woman dragged Sere from rack to rack until her arms were filled with the trappings of the new persona. "A wide-brimmed sun hat would be just perfect—"

"I think I'm good," Sere interjected. "I'll just pay and be on my way."

"Don't be silly. You simply must try it all on. I'm dying to see what you look like all dressed up."

Keep pestering me, and dying *will be the operative word,* Sere thought. "I'm really in a bit of a hurry."

The woman shrugged as if she couldn't fathom why Sere was being so rude as to deny her the pleasure of seeing her creation come to life. "If you must. You can pay Emily at the counter." She turned away like a lover scorned and headed back to the entrance for her next fashion victim.

With the oversized shopping bag designed to advertise to every mall patron that Village Vintage Attire had made another sale, Sere navigated the shortest possible route back to her motorcycle. As she passed the sports bar, she caught the grating voice of the news reporter. "This just in. The police believe the woman in question might be riding a vintage motorcycle."

Shit!

8

From what little Sere knew of women her age, she suspected she might be the only one on earth not to own a cell phone. The damn things hadn't existed when she was born in the 1800s. While in hell, she'd relied on the interdimensional gates to talk to the handful of people in life who were important to her. Now that she'd made it to the land of the living, the fucking blocks of technology were about as useful for communication as bricks. For the first time in her odd life, she wished she had some way to keep tabs on the information that streamed to every passerby.

Back out in the parking lot, she opened her saddlebags and coaxed her snakes out of the way so she could add in the shopping bags filled with the trappings of her new identity. "With no way for me to contact them, I guess Aunt Kendell and Uncle Myles are just going to have to deal with me showing up out of the blue. If they're too busy or can't find room for me, I'm sure we can find some empty lot to set up for the night. I know you guys would be more comfortable if we were all outside, anyway." The snakes started their rattles of displeasure at the threat of being kept indoors. "Just be glad you don't have to hide your true identities. You'd look pretty stupid in wigs and sunglasses." *Not that I look much better.*

Though it was potentially dangerous taking off her disguise in the vicinity of Jennifer and having her likeness plastered all over the news, Sere couldn't safely operate the Triton with it on. She caressed the handlebars, fearing she wouldn't be able to use her trusty motorcycle for much longer. Eventually, all the paranoid chicken-shit city slickers would start reporting every woman on two wheels. According to the overly enthusiastic bubbleheaded reporter, however, the killing spree was still happening well outside New Orleans. *"The police chief wants to make it clear: the people of New Orleans have nothing to fear."*

Sere grumbled, "She could have tried a little harder to make it sound like she believed what she was reading. God, I want to slap that sensationalist reporting bitch." Sere kicked over the Triton's motor, imagining that the starter lever was the newswoman's face, and headed back to the freeway.

With each mile closer to the heart of the city, more cars crowded around her on the freeway—each one filled with people. *Stop imagining every person you pass is staring at you. Even if the news weren't broadcasting your picture, you'd still feel vehicular claustrophobia.*

At the freeway interchange, most of the traffic veered right toward the Quarter and Central Business District. Sere headed left. Before she braved the center of tourist activity to fulfill her pseudo-familial obligation to Kendell and Myles, she needed to learn a little more about defeating Monty. She tucked in behind a tractor trailer that took an off-ramp leading to the wharfs along the Mississippi. Free from the barrage of passenger vehicles loaded with tourists having nothing better to do than stare at the chick on the motorcycle, Sere's panic subsided. The narrow access roads sucked with their potholes, poorly marked cross streets, and coned-off repairs, but at least on her motorcycle, she had the maneuverability to avoid most of the obstacles, even if the giant trucks made it impossible to pass.

THE GRAVEL ROAD to the far end of the docks was so seldom used that weeds had crept in from the neighboring abandoned lot. Sere edged her motorcycle along the path, trying to keep the dust from announcing her arrival. When she came to the end, she got off her bike and walked it out to the mostly deserted shipping offices.

"I suppose this is as good a time as any to get used to my disguise." She quickly took off her helmet and pulled on her wig to avoid being noticed. A snake uncoiled from under the artificial hair, slithered down in front of her face, turned its beady little eyes to her, and stuck out its tongue. "Damn it, snake, this isn't a medusa wig. That's not funny." She lifted the serpent off her forehead and let it curl back into the saddlebag. It dove under the clothes as if giving her the cold shoulder. "Okay, it was a little funny in a very Greek-mythology kind of way." The canebrake gave a dismissive flick of its last rattle as it disappeared into the pant leg of her spare pair of jeans. Snakes could be so sensitive.

She put on the oversized sunglasses and checked her appearance in the motorcycle's side mirror. "I still look ridiculous." She threw the saddlebags over her shoulder and headed to the front of the office that faced the river.

As she pushed open the plywood-covered glass door, the old man in the Barcalounger said, "Hello, Sere," without turning to face her.

"You could have at least looked at my disguise before dashing my hopes of anonymity."

The chair's leather groaned as Professor Yates stood up. "And lie to you? What good would that have done?" He pointed to a bank of computer monitors that lined one wall of the small office. "Besides, I knew you were coming from half a mile away."

View screens compared Sere's disguised face with projections that were continually updating her doppelgänger body. "I guess it's fairly easy for you to figure out who's who in hell."

He stood beside her, looking over his work. "These computer banks hold images of every person who's wandered New Orleans for the last twenty years. Each doppelgänger is modeled and projected based on those files, so matching one of you up is pretty straightforward no matter the attempted disguise."

"I guess it's a good thing you're on my side." *And a good thing the loas are technologically naïve.* She wasn't going to share that last thought with Professor Yates. Even though he was as aware of Sere's situation with the afterlife as anyone, she still didn't like broadcasting her fears.

He turned to her and puffed up his chest like a proud grandfather. "You're all that matters."

The computer screens were doing much more than identifying Sere. Views of the hell dimension filled most of the wall. "Is that why you don't just shut off this virtual-reality diorama? All this is just to keep me going?" She had trouble accepting that so much danger was kept running simply so her odd existence was allowed to continue. With a quick flip of the switch, Monty would be no more.

"We love you, child, but even you aren't that important. Twenty years ago, your father turned loose an energy chain reaction that ran between our two dimensions. The only way to utilize the power and prevent a runaway condition that could doom us all was to build this contraption. Hell has to exist even if there aren't any souls kept prisoner there."

Except Sanguine, Sere thought, but this wasn't the time to worry about her surrogate mother. "But why the emergency doppelgänger-warning device?"

"When you were just a girl and your father stepped out of his prison dimension to face his demise, I suspected the day would come when another denizen of hell would come looking for me, so I stashed some sensors around my lair just to be prepared."

She set her saddlebags on his desk. History was only interesting if it gave her something to use in the present. "I need a place to stash my stuff while I'm in the city. I also need to understand more about who I'm hunting."

"Straight to it. I've always liked that about you. Though I guess later you'll be dealing with enough small talk with Kendell and Myles to last a lifetime."

"Don't remind me." She took off Joe's jacket, yanked the shotgun from the holster on her back, and set them next to her saddlebags. She then pulled her dress out of her bag. "I fucking hate this thing, but I need to get used to looking like a lady."

He snickered at the unusual attire and pointed down the hallway. "There's a bathroom halfway down the hall. Mind telling me how you're going to hide that shotgun while wearing a dress?"

"If I'm right about Monty still figuring out how to efficiently kill a person, he'll be a few days from entering New Orleans to confront his real. I should have some time to get ready for him. Wandering around the Quarter in bike leathers with a shotgun concealed on my back would be a bit conspicuous in this summer heat."

He pulled a ring of keys out from the desk. "While you're getting changed, I'll wheel your motorcycle into the storage room in the back. Then we can have a chat about what to do with this demon from hell."

~

SERE HAD NEVER UNDERSTOOD why some women took

forever to get themselves dressed and presentable. As she stood inspecting herself in the bathroom mirror, however, she wondered how she'd find the nerve to set foot outside Professor Yates's offices. From wig to sneakers, each part of her disguise felt about to slip right off and reveal the murderess described on the newscasts. *I need to start paying attention to what the authorities have found. Maybe I'll get lucky and they'll kill Monty in a shootout. More likely, they'll shoot him full of holes only to discover he can't be killed.* She readjusted the wig for the tenth time.

The bangs fell below the tops of the sunglasses. The fake hair teased her eyebrows under the thick frames. "Well, at least no one will recognize me."

She gave up and left the bathroom, haunted by a feeling of being like a girl going trick-or-treating in whatever she could steal from her mother's closet. Jennifer's memories— which had a way of surfacing when they were least wanted —didn't help Sere's evaluation of the costume. Professor Yates stood in the middle of the office, wearing a broad smile, his hand on what looked like a vehicle for a child.

"What is that thing?"

He turned the handlebars so she could get a better look. "It's a motor scooter."

From the way he presented it, she assumed he meant it for her. "What do you expect me to do with it?"

"You ride it. You can't exactly go tearing through the Quarter on your café racer while wearing a dress."

She set her folded jeans, halter top, and boots next to her saddlebags. "I thought everyone walked in New Orleans."

He shrugged and started pushing the scooter back

toward the hallway. "If you don't want it, I'll put it away. I just thought you might appreciate the mobility."

"Stop." She squeezed her eyes closed, realizing she'd been insensitive. "Of course I want it. Thank you." The final two words felt like some foreign language she didn't speak fluently.

"I know it doesn't fit your usual badass persona, but trust me, you'll fit right in puttering around on this relic." He set the scooter on its kickstand next to the door.

She pulled the dagger from her boot, which was on the table. "At least I can strap this to my leg. You wouldn't happen to have a standard ace bandage or something I could use as a holster, would you?"

He nodded toward the back room. "Joe keeps a stash of emergency supplies back there. I'm sure you can find plenty of holsters and weapons in his footlocker. Now, how can I help you deal with this doppelgänger?"

She sat at the desk and pulled out a box of shells Andy had prepared from the backpack. "I know I can kill Monty by shooting him with one of these or cutting his head off. Anything else I do to him will just make for a bloody mess that I'll have to explain while he regenerates and makes another attack. The clock is ticking. I have to get to him before he kills his real or people figure out that there are two Montgomery Fishers running around town. What don't I know?"

Professor Yates lit his pipe and settled back into his lounge chair. "There has always been the threat that a doppelgänger might meet its real."

Though Professor Yates was responsible for Sere's

continued existence, she wasn't comfortable telling him she'd already crossed that line. "What about a doppelgänger meeting a different real? Would the copy know what was discussed with the real?"

"Are you thinking of confronting Mr. Fisher in person?"

Sere shrugged. "I could say I was looking for some tax advice."

"You haven't worked a day in your life. You'd look like a little girl asking what she owed the government from her allowance."

"Speaking of which, you wouldn't happen to have some cash you could spare?" She lifted the hem of her flower-print dress. "I spent my last twenty on this frock."

"You got ripped off." He reached into his jeans pocket and pulled out a worn leather wallet. "I've got a hundred fifteen bucks. It's all yours." He put the bills on the desk.

"Thanks." *So this is what it feels like to be a girl asking her father for money. Fuck this. Next time, I'll steal what I need.* Sere folded the bills and thrust them into the dress pocket. "I'm not even sure what I'd say to Mr. Fisher, but as Monty's real, he might give me some insight into where Monty might go first on entering New Orleans."

Professor Yates set his pipe in an ashtray on the desk. "I hear Joe's training kicking in. You're looking for some weakness in Mr. Fisher that Monty might not even suspect in himself. Just don't let on about the whole doppelgänger thing. Even if he brushed the idea off, people have a way of letting such notions fester."

"But if I tell him his life is in danger," Sere said, "he might be able to be prepared."

"Play the idea out, though. Even if he does take you seriously, it's unlikely he'd call the cops based on some wild girl's warning. As a Southerner with more than a little money, Mr. Fisher undoubtedly has a gun or two. So he stays armed just in case you are correct. Then we have the inevitable shoot-out between doppelgänger and real."

Sere raised her hand for the professor to stop. "You've made your point. Mr. Fisher loses that battle, the loas get involved, and the police show up to find the carnage of one dead and one immortal version of the same dude."

Professor Yates waved at his banks of computers. "I've had nineteen years to worry. No matter how I run the scenarios, if two versions of the same person ever meet, eventually our secret gets out. So long as there's a separation between dimensions, my computer programs work like check valves. I can project this reality into hell and prevent hell from seeping back. The real people outside that door have no idea they have duplicates in hell. If a doppelgänger crosses over, however, and meets its real, their shared consciousness is like pouring oil and water into the same pot. They remain separate, but a certain amount of mixing of knowledge is inevitable."

Shit! Hopefully, those around Jennifer would believe she had a vivid imagination—though Sere doubted Jenny had enough brainpower for true creativity.

She changed the subject to something less condemning and more useful in her quest. "How about those sensors of yours? Is there a way we could set them up around Mr. Fisher's office or home?"

"We'd run the risk of someone stumbling on them and figuring out that doppelgängers are among us."

"Sounds like I'm on my own." *I should have just stayed on the hunt.* She tried to remain stoic, Joe's first rule ringing in her head as if she'd been hit with it by a baseball bat: no self-pity.

"That's not true. You've got Joe's training. Kendell and Myles are respected members of the community. They have ties among every economic stratum that they can call on for help. I may not be much use in a fight, but I can offer you these offices, where you'll be safe. Figure out what you need. We'll all be here for you."

THE MOST IMPORTANT thing Sere took from her meeting with Professor Yates was also the most obvious: she needed a plan. But any coordinated effort required knowing the strengths and weaknesses of those closest to her. She could walk into any bar and quickly identify every potential threat and possible weapon, but reading the abilities of those she'd need to rely on wasn't so easy. Leaning on others required trust, and that wasn't a condition Sere found comfortable. The difference between people was like choosing an oak chair over one made of pine. They both looked and functioned pretty much the same for their stated purpose. The only way to discover which was more useful in a fight was to actually bust someone over the head with the two and see which splintered to pieces and which laid out the adversary. Evaluating a person's usefulness, however, often required making the assessment without the benefit of combat.

Night had fallen by the time she left Professor Yates's offices. Without her gun, motorcycle, or snakes, she felt more vulnerable than she wanted to admit. She ran a hand along the side of her dress to assure herself that the knife strapped to her leg was easily accessible. Sitting sidesaddle on the small, rattly scooter with her legs exposed didn't help her self-image as a badass demon hunter. At the moderate speed, at least, her wig didn't blow out of place. Her dress flapped around her legs as she gave the scooter full throttle. *I guess a bar fight is out of the question tonight.* Not that she wanted to bust up Aunt Kendell and Uncle Myles's establishment, but some activities had a way of happening in spite of her intentions.

As a challenge to her nerves, she headed up Esplanade. Sanguine's ghost stories about deranged doppelgängers out to steal young Sere's body parts always took place between the elegant tree-lined avenue and Canal Street, two roads that helped define the trapezoidal nightmare of the French Quarter. *Come and get me, assholes,* she thought. But the only people she passed were bands of gutter punks and laughing tourists. She looked at the drunk, giggling fools and wondered, *Why did I think reals here would have more depth than their doppelgängers in hell?*

She turned right onto Royal Street, away from the Quarter and toward Frenchmen Street and the Scratchy Dog. The throngs of hipsters, fashionable tourists, street musicians, and all manner of artists plying their creativity on every street corner made it nearly impossible to maneuver the small scooter down the narrow, crowded road. She set the faded-yellow motorbike on its stand behind a black VW bus covered in white Dia de los Muertos images. The fanciful skulls had her shaking her head. *Like that's what the dead look like. Someone's clearly never been to hell.*

She squeezed past a group of excited women holding red plastic cups filled with alcohol so strong it made Sere's eyes water. *This is insane. I'm never getting into the club, and even if I do, Aunt Kendell and Uncle Myles are going to be way too busy. I'm letting my experiences from hell get the better of me. Reals can't drop everything and pay attention to me just because I ask.*

With each step farther into the throng of people, Sere's sense of panic increased. Like a salmon struggling to spawn upstream only to discover it had made a wrong turn, Sere turned around and fought against the mindless mass's attempt at forcing her to join the mob. The claustrophobia of so many bodies pressed around her caused her heart to race. Without an adversary to confront, the fight-or-flight impulse had only one outlet. She put her palms flat together and cut like a fish through the gaggle of drunk women intent on pressing their way into the club. Once past the pheromone-fueled females, Sere eased up on her struggle, but the need to run—which she had seldom before experienced—didn't abate until she rounded a corner into a dark side street. The seclusion that most women feared, she found comforting. But the confusing maze of streets that met at oblique angles made it impossible to figure out a direct path back to the scooter. Groups of partiers noisily passed her as she turned down one street then the next.

As she sought out a street sign for some hint of her location, a thin-bladed knife penetrated deep into her back. *Fuck. This is what I get for allowing myself to become distracted.* She resisted the urge to summersault away from her assailant and have it out in the street. Too many people might be attracted by the scuffle like moths to the flame. *If any of them gets killed in the fight, the loas will be all over my ass.*

The man behind her turned the knife to direct her like she was an insect impaled on a pin. "Walk nice and slow. We're just two people looking for a quiet corner to get to know each other better." He drove the blade in so deep she could feel his fist on the handle against her back.

"What do you want with me? Please don't hurt me." She did her best to add some trembling to her voice. If her abductor thought she was scared, she might be able to catch him off guard.

He nudged her toward a deserted side street. "I think we both know a little knife isn't going to do you much damage, Sere Mal-Laurette. Though I am curious: if cutting off your head is the only way to kill you, what happens if I sever your spine?"

"So you know who I am." She gave up the pretense of fear. Anyone who knew her wouldn't be so easily fooled into thinking she was a damsel in distress. "If you expected me to keep walking, I wouldn't do any additional damage if I were you."

He clicked a remote inside his pants. The sliding door of a van in front of her opened as if by magic. He yanked the knife out of her and kneed her in the small of her back. She fell face-first onto a blue tarp that covered the floor of the van. Her black wig flew off her head and landed in a corner like a scared dog scampering for safety.

Rolling onto her side, Sere was finally able to face her enemy. "Thomas?" Though the boy lab assistant was now a man, Sere easily remembered the facial features of the doppelgänger she'd decapitated as a girl. He slammed the door shut before she could reach for her blade.

9

"*I* don't have time for this bullshit." The van's walls rumbled like someone shaking a piece of sheet metal to imitate the sound of thunder. "Can you not hit *every* fucking pothole?" Sere couldn't reach the wound on her back to stop the bleeding. It stung like blazes, but as deep as it was, it would heal on its own eventually. Passing out from blood loss, however, was a real possibility, and that was going to make it hard to fight. She wouldn't give him the satisfaction of expressing fear or pain. "Are we there yet? I have to pee."

"Just shut up. You're in no position to counterattack. By the time we get where we're going, the blood loss should make you nice and docile."

"I wouldn't count on me being nice regardless of my physical condition." *Fucking real Thomas is even more annoying than his doppelgänger.* She needed to keep him talking. So long as he thought he was in charge, she might get him to say something useful. "I won't do you much good while comatose, so how about answering some of my questions as a way of keeping me conscious?" He swung the van violently to the right, which forced her to roll onto the gaping wound. *You fucking did that on purpose.*

"I suppose it couldn't hurt."

"How do you know about me?" From the increase in speed, she assumed they'd gotten onto a main road. The smoother ride allowed her to sit upright against the van's wall and get a glimpse out the windshield.

"When you chopped off my shadow's head, I gained his memories. At first I thought they were just my teenaged delusions, but as I grew older, his thoughts became a part of my own."

"That's not possible." The pain in Sere's back was nothing compared to the shocking revelation. *That fucking arrogant professor and his toys.*

"I don't make the rules."

"Even if you do know what I did, how did you know how to find me?" Her disguise might not have been the best, but to someone who must have thought he was dreaming up a murderess, it should have sufficed.

"I have my sources."

And if one of those sources happens to be in hell, I'll have to add another tick to my suspicion column regarding someone playing games in hell. "Still getting messages from the beyond? I would have thought without your doppelgänger, you would be happy to be rid of hell."

"You don't know shit about hell."

By flexing her legs, she forced her back firmly against

the metal wall to stop the bleeding. "Bullshit. You're just trying to get under my skin. I lived most of my life in hell."

He slammed on the brakes so hard she tumbled up against the barrier behind the front seats. He then turned on her with a glare she'd never seen from a living human being. "You honestly believe you experienced hell? That dimension was your playground, and you acted like a spoiled little girl ripping the heads off her dolls."

The blood oozing from her back soaked her dress from bra to panties. Consciousness threatened to drain out of her like water swirling out of a claw-foot tub. *I have to stay focused.* "You can't possibly be this obsessed with me harming what was little more than your virtual-reality avatar."

"It was all just a game to you, wasn't it? You really don't get it. I was a nice guy before I bonded with my hell persona. People liked me. I had a girlfriend, a steady job, a future. Now I'm an asshole. The former me wouldn't have even thought about abducting you, let alone running a knife into you. Who I am now, however, will happily kill you and not even lose any sleep over the murder."

She still had her knife. He'd gotten the drop on her by using the crowd, but he hadn't killed her when he had the chance. The evil he saw in himself hadn't fully taken over. Unlike Monty, Thomas did have a soul that rejected the impulse to kill. His inexperience with evil gave her the advantage. He was counting on her loss of blood making her unable to fight. She just needed to string him along for a little longer. *I still need to find out who's involved. But equally important, I need to find out if killing a doppelgänger releases its evil into its real—and if so, what will happen when I do in Monty the serial killer. I need to study this deranged hybrid.*

Thomas got out and opened the sliding door. "Let's go."

She rolled to her side and spoke in a broken whisper. "I don't think I can."

He bent into the van and wrapped an arm around her waist. As he hauled her from the vehicle, she slipped his switchblade out of his belt and stashed it in her dress. She let her feet drag against the pavement while he struggled to maneuver her weakened body into the garage warehouse.

He gently lowered her into the desk chair. "I suppose you're not a threat. Don't do anything stupid, and I won't tie you up."

She made a show of trying to breathe in enough air to compensate for the hole in her lung. "So are you going to kill me now? Have you thought this through? For starters, my blood is on your knife, in your van, and soaked into your clothing. People might not have seen you stab me, but someone is sure to have noticed you toss me into your vehicle. Just having the impulse to kill isn't the same as knowing how to get away with it."

Thomas stood over her with his arms crossed like an asshole ex-boyfriend about to accuse her of an indiscretion. "If I wanted to kill you, I wouldn't have gone to the trouble of abducting you. You put this evil in me. You can damn well figure out a way to get it out."

At least you're not asking me to make you immortal, she thought. "I can talk to the professor, but as your doppelgänger used to work for him, you could do that yourself."

"And once again be that old man's lab rat? I don't think so. Besides, he's just the architect of hell. You may not be the gatekeeper, but you know who is. I hold you personally responsible for the evil within me. Figure out how to remove it from me, and return it to hell where it belongs."

She coughed up blood and spit it on the concrete floor. The metallic taste of iron and copper made it hard to breathe without gagging. "I get it, but what do you expect me to do? We're not talking about you being possessed. Your doppelgänger was based on who you are. It's not my fault you can't face your personal demons."

"Subject anyone to hell for long enough, and they're bound to turn dark and twisted."

Sere had had just about enough of Thomas's whining. *I've already got a goddamned mass murderer to contend with.* "I'm not your fucking demonic psychiatrist."

Thomas moved in menacingly. When he reached for the knife that wasn't there, Sere made her move. With one foot, she kicked hard against the heavy wooden chair, sending it flying backward toward the wall. Using the momentum, she lunged forward, pulled her knife from under her dress and his from her pocket and, like an expert assassin, held the two blades to his throat—one at the front and one at the back. The artery in his neck pulsed against the razor-sharp steel.

"I could free you of your evil with little more than a paper cut," she said. "I was only a kid when I beheaded your doppelgänger, but even back then, he was a better adversary than you are now. Did you really think you could outmaneuver me?" Her adrenaline made up for her blood loss. Though there wasn't a bullet holding the puncture open as with her last injury, the dirt and fabric from her dress prevented her flesh from bonding shut. In the exhilaration of battle, she drew even more energy from her real. *I hope Jennifer drank lots of liquids today. She's going to need it to replace the energy I'm draining.*

Thomas cringed as he swallowed. His Adam's apple bobbed dangerously hard against the sharp metal. "Please don't kill me."

"I don't like being stabbed, abducted, or threatened. Don't do it again. Now, how exactly did you find me?"

He pointed at the cell phone in his pocket. "My shadow helped Professor Yates develop the doppelgänger detection system. Once my evil twin joined me, I was able to simplify the technology to a smart-phone app."

Peachy. Another bit of technology that won't do me a damn bit of good. "So you just happened to be standing in the right place at the right time when your phone vibrated in your pants? Then you whipped out your knife like some flasher displaying his cock and rammed it in the first woman who passed by? I'm not buying it."

"I got a notification when the professor's detection system went off. I could see his computer screens on my phone, so I knew who you really were. I saw you walk up to his office in your riding attire and motorcycle and leave in that dress, pushing a scooter. My smart-phone app tracks you like you were wearing a GPS chip. It didn't take a genius to figure out you'd visit your surrogate family eventually. With the crowds, Frenchmen Street was the least conspicuous place for me to lie in wait."

Sere could feel each hard breath he took against her knife. "So you're saying you didn't have help? Because if this is all just you, I have no reason not to slit your throat."

"Don't do it, Sere."

Hearing Kendell's voice at the door made Sere instinctively flex her arms and force the blades harder against Thomas's throat. A trickle of blood ran along the edge to the hilt.

"How did you find me?" she growled at Kendell between clenched teeth.

"Joe told us you were in town," Kendell said. "You parked my old scooter near the band's van. Professor Yates told me you'd borrowed it. Since we didn't see you at the club, we figured there must have been a problem—"

"Please stop," Sere interrupted. "I'm sorry I asked." Life-and-death situations weren't the time for long-winded answers to pointless mysteries.

"Just put the knives down," Myles said in what was probably supposed to be an authoritative tone but sounded more like a councilor talking someone off a ledge.

Sere refocused her attention on the two blades poised like scissors about to clip off Thomas's head. "Not until he learns his lesson."

He stared into her eyes. "If you're not going to help me, then go ahead and kill me. I can't live like this any longer." She could see from his unflinching gaze that he was serious.

You're not a killer. As the adrenaline drained from her system, she remembered the intellectual exercise she'd conducted on the ride down to New Orleans. "Don't cross my path again, and I'll see what I can do. If I see you again, I will kill you." Even drawing on Jennifer's life force had its limits. Now that she had Thomas at her mercy, she no longer had the thrill of the fight to keep her energized. She'd gotten what information she could out of him, and he wasn't in a position to resume his threat. Reluctantly, she lowered her blades.

Thomas backed slowly away while still facing Sere, as if he couldn't believe she was going to let him live. With each step he took, she calculated how much strength it would take to throw the dagger into his heart.

~

SERE SHOOK her head in disbelief when Myles and Kendell helped her outside to the black VW bus with white sugar skulls. *Of course it belongs to you two.* The blue tarp that had covered the back of Thomas's van lay in a heap next to the back door.

"I guess he didn't want to drive around with the incriminating evidence," Sere said. "At least that should keep me from getting blood all over those Mexican blankets."

Kendell stuck close to Sere's side like an overly protective mother hen while Myles spread the plastic-impregnated cloth inside the old bus. "We can take you to Professor Yates. He can hook you up—"

"No." One intense connection to Jennifer in a week was more than enough. "Just take me somewhere I can get cleaned up. The wound looks more dramatic than it is." She still felt lightheaded from the blood loss. Though she could draw on Jennifer's healing energy to speed the process, blood and tissue still needed to be regenerated by her own body. With no direct threat, she preferred to do the work herself.

Myles turned and jiggled the key in the VW's ignition as if unlocking a Japanese puzzle box. The ignition finally engaged, creating a loud backfire before the old engine settled down to its rhythmic rattling. "We'll take you back to our place. It's not much, but you'll be safe."

Sere faded in and out of consciousness during the short ride. Each time she felt the warm embrace of sleep coming on, Kendell grabbed her hand to bring her back to reality.

"Honestly, I'll be fine. I've suffered worse." Sere didn't mention that her last injury had been recent. There was no need to add to their concern for her.

"It makes me feel better knowing you're still with us," Kendell said.

"At least I'm not being tossed around like a rag doll. From now on, I think I'll stick to my motorcycle for transportation." Leaving her fate in the hands of another driver felt like giving up all her autonomy. Every block they drove past Esplanade into the Quarter made her skin crawl, which didn't help with healing the gash in her back. Fortunately, the ride didn't last long.

Kendell helped her out of the van and up the stairs to their apartment. Once the need for physical exertion had passed, her body experienced the damage Thomas's knife had inflicted. Sere fell onto the ottoman between two attentive pups.

"Wait here for a minute, and I'll get a bath going for you," Kendell said.

With her blood-soaked dress, disheveled hair lacking the wig, and as much spent adrenaline as blood pumping through her veins, Sere felt acutely out of place. In an attempt at easing her discomfort, she patted the heads of the two Lhasa apsos that lay on either side of her. "How old are your dogs?" Casual conversation had never felt more out of place, but at least it was a distraction from her condition.

Myles pulled a bottle of Jameson's from the cupboard. "Cheesecake is thirty-four, and Doughnut Hole is twenty-one."

Sere stared into the older dog's eyes. "I know I haven't spent much time in this reality, but I didn't think that kind of age was possible for a dog." The mutt still had the alertness of a puppy.

"Their longevity was payment from Papa Ghede for dealing with your father." Myles handed Sere a glass filled two fingers high with whiskey.

She turned the clear tumbler with the amber liquid in her hand. "How did you know?"

"A good bartender or an attentive gentleman never forgets a lady's drink preference."

She tossed the whiskey back with one gulp. The familiar smooth vanilla flavor and floral bouquet were drowned out by the metallic taste of blood that still filled her mouth and sinuses.

Myles refilled her glass as soon as she lowered it from her mouth. "After the last couple of days you've had, no one's going to judge you for going on a bit of a bender tonight. You're safe here."

She sipped the second drink. "I'm not a friendly drunk—usually there's carnage involved."

He sat on the sofa and set the bottle on the side table. "Like up in Jackson's Bluff?"

"That was different. I was soliciting information."

"Is that also what you were doing with Thomas?" Myles asked. "Because if so, we might want to work on your investigative style." He hid his smirk behind a sip of whiskey.

She turned her back to him so he could see the gash that ripped through her dress clear to her exposed ribs. "He had it coming."

Kendell saved Myles from receiving more of Sere's cuttingly witty sarcasm by emerging from the hallway. "I've got everything ready. Let's get you out of those clothes and cleaned up."

"I keep telling you, I'm fine on my own."

From Kendell's scowl, Sere knew she was in for a fight, and unlike a physical altercation, it would be a battle she wasn't likely to win.

"I'm fully aware of your interdimensional situation," Kendell said. "I helped create it. You may be a badass, but you know better than to cross me."

Only Sanguine could really control Sere, but as the guardian angel's sister in the paranormal, Auntie Kendell came in a close second. Poor Joe was a distant third, having to rely on physical strength rather than rapier wit.

"I suppose I could use some help cleaning the wound," Sere said. "It is a little hard to reach."

Kendell softened her strict stance by uncoiling her arms

from her chest. She took Sere by the hand as if she were a little girl who'd gotten hurt playing outdoors. "Bring your drink. We need to get all of the foreign material out of that wound. Even with your kickass attitude, it's going to hurt."

Sere wanted to explain how many times she'd been in worse situations, but making Kendell turn green from the stories wasn't likely to give the woman the fortitude to do the necessary work. "Lead the way."

Sere stepped into the bathroom, expecting it to be covered in plastic like a murderer's kill room. With the trail of blood that dripped off her dress, she wouldn't have blamed Kendell for trying to keep their home from looking like a crime scene. To her surprise, the small but luxurious bathroom smelled of vanilla from the softly burning scented candles. A thick towel was laid over the lip of the sink and another on the edge of the deep tub, which was filled with swirling water. Kendell touched Sere's shoulders and started peeling off the rags that just that afternoon had been a polka-dotted sundress. Drying blood bonded the fabric to her skin like glue.

Sere tried to reach up to help, but Kendell swatted her hand away. "Just relax, for a change, and let me take care of you. Put your hands on the sides of the sink, and lean over so I can attend to that gash. It looks awfully deep."

Sere pulled Thomas's knife out of her dress pocket before Kendell managed to yank the mess of fabric past her breasts and unhooked her bra. She set the blade in the sink to be cleaned. "I don't need to be stitched up."

Kendell pressed a hot towel into the wound. From the sting, Sere assumed there was some antibiotic cleaning agent involved. "I'm fully aware of your physiology. All I'm going to do is get out the dirt and fabric. Then I'll tape a dressing over it so you can bathe without pain or recontamination. By the time you rejoin us, I'm sure you'll be as good as new and just as feisty."

After years of training, Sere didn't really know how to let down her guard. Being continually prepared for battle meant certain muscles in her arms and shoulders hadn't relaxed in a decade. Kendell's firm, caring touch on Sere's back was like having Lefty's scutes massage it.

"I think that will do it," Kendell said. "Can you feel anything in your back that shouldn't be there? I can go deeper."

Sere shed the remainder of her blood-soaked clothing so she could stand upright. Her muscles resumed their standard tension of preparedness. With only her knife sheathed against her thigh, her reflection in the mirror looked ready to resume the battle. "I think you got it."

Kendell wadded up the blood-soaked towels and garments and stashed them in a black garbage bag. "I set some clothes out on our bed. My jeans might be a little loose on you, and I can't vouch for the condition of Myles's cotton shirt. If they don't work for you, rummage around until you find something that fits. Enjoy the bath for as long as you like. Please use anything you find in this apartment as if it were your own."

Sere unstrapped the knife holster and set it and the blade on the counter next to the sink. "Thank you, Auntie Kendell."

~

ONCE KENDELL HAD LEFT the bathroom, Sere picked up her glass of whiskey and eyed the tub with trepidation. Luxury had a way of being more addictive than alcohol. Joe always said soldiers in the field never let down their guard, and Sere had enemies both known and unknown to contend with. For all of her adult life, bathing had involved cold and often murky water shared with other creatures. The deep jet tub filled with water contaminated only with bath salts felt like a well-baited trap.

She took a long swig of her drink. "I'm being foolish. I'll never be as safe as I am right now. It could be months before I'll once again be able to truly get all the grunge off me." She stepped into the hot swirling water and set her glass on the tiled enclosure surrounding the tub. Easing into the water felt like the equivalent of downing a glass of Jameson in one gulp. The warmth soothed every nerve ending.

Memories of the first seven years of Serephine Malveaux's life came flooding back. Archibald Malveaux had more than his share of faults, but as a young girl, Serephine had been kept in the dark regarding her father's activities. The hot bath reminded her of a warm antebellum afternoon. Her mother had been combing out Serephine's long gossamer hair while the girl lounged in the mansion's copper tub. The humid, fragrant New Orleans air seemed to meld right into the bathwater.

In Sere's hazy memory, a wild man had burst into the house. "Your husband has stolen my family!" he yelled at

Serephine's mother. The man looked to have spent the last week sleeping in the gutter. His once-fashionable suit was ripped and soaked. He smelled of rotting meat, alcohol, and vomit. All young Serephine could think was, *Why has this crazy man interrupted my bath time?*

"Please, not in front of my daughter." Her mother's voice quivered. Serephine had never heard her sound like that.

"Why not?" the man yelled. "What about my daughters, who are about to be prostitutes in your husband's brothels? Is your sweet, innocent child somehow more precious than my own? I curse you all for letting him get away with this evil."

Sere hadn't understood all of the man's words back then, but the fear in his voice had made her shiver in spite of the hot water and sultry afternoon. It was as if the world's cold reality had just been dumped on top of her. The little girl was forced to grow up in an instant.

Sere stopped the memory like a projectionist holding a film reel's single frame under a magnifying lens. The man's penetrating brown eyes, high cheekbones, and jet-black hair were all too familiar. Kendell's great-great-grandfather was no less passionate about those he loved than Kendell herself, whose lineage was woven into Sere's.

"You just had to fuck the man's daughters, didn't you, father? All the women and girls you could get your hands on became your indentured concubines—stolen from their families as payment for loans you knew their men couldn't pay. How many of New Orleans's high-class families have you destroyed and bound to me because of your lusts?"

Sere drained the last of her Jameson's as a means of

bringing her thoughts back to the present. "I suppose it's more like Illegitimate-Half-Niece-Multiple-Times-Removed Kendell, but *Auntie* feels like a more appropriate title. Given enough family history, I suppose we're all interrelated somehow."

She lounged back in the fiberglass tub with the empty glass still in her hand and drifted off to sleep.

∼

SERE WOKE the next morning on the living room couch with Doughnut Hole licking her face. She vaguely remembered getting out of the lukewarm water, dressing, and rejoining Kendell and Myles after her bath the night before. As with most conversations that didn't directly pertain to her mission, she'd only half tuned in to what they'd said. Their one useful tidbit of information was that three more people had gone missing along the route from Jackson's Bluff to New Orleans, bringing the number of likely homicides to seven. The fact that there were no signs of human remains led Sere to believe Monty had graduated from amateur murderer to full-blown psycho killer.

Kendell and Myles had gone to bed soon after being convinced Sere was fine and wasn't going to sneak out in the early-morning hours to go hunting the demon without first saying goodbye. She picked up the small black dog and stared into his black eyes. "I'm awake. You can stop now."

He gave her a playful bark. When she set him down, he made a beeline for the back bedroom. *Great. Now I'll have to resume the mindless conversation. I need to keep it short so I can get back to the hunt for Monty. Yesterday's distraction has put me seriously behind.* Not that Kendell and Myles weren't pleasant enough, but sooner or later, they would offer to help—or worse, ask about Sanguine.

"You look like a new woman." Kendell followed the two dogs into the living room, wearing a thick robe.

"I hope I didn't keep you up too late. The need for things like sleep and food still mystify me."

Kendell headed into the kitchen and started a pot of coffee. "Don't worry about us. As club owners, Myles and I keep pretty unusual hours. How are you feeling?"

Sere got up from the couch, reached for the ceiling, and stretched out her back. Every muscle was working as intended. "All better."

The harsh stare from under Kendell's brow indicated she wasn't completely convinced, but Sere didn't press the issue. "What are your plans?"

"I'm not going to kill Montgomery Fisher, if that's what you're asking. I do need to meet with him, however. The more I understand about his life, the easier it will be for me to intercept his doppelgänger."

"We can go with you. As business owners, we can say we're in the market for a new accountant. That should at least get you in the door."

There it is—less than five minutes before she offered to help. "I don't need a chaperone."

"Maybe not, but you will be walking through the Quarter." Kendell grabbed her oversized handbag from the counter and pulled out Sere's wig and glasses. "Myles found these in the blue tarp when he cleaned out the VW. He disposed of everything covered in blood."

Sere's heart started fluttering. "I hope he did a thorough job of it. Those blood-soaked items could lead the police back to you. If they figure out that Thomas was involved and start questioning him, he might put you two in a lot of trouble to save his hide and maintain whatever hold he thinks he has on me." *Worrying about you is really not what I need right now.*

Kendell handed her a cup of steaming coffee. "We're not that naïve. Don't forget, we were the ones who introduced you to Joe Cazenave. We have resources you couldn't imagine."

"The last two people who helped me are both dead. I won't risk your lives."

Kendell sat with her overweight dog while the younger black pup headed back to the bedroom. "We do have more than a little experience facing danger."

Sere sat on the sofa and leaned in toward Kendell. "Not like this. Don't get me wrong. What you did in containing and defeating the devil was amazing, but we're not talking spells and attempted redemption this time. Monty has one goal, and that's to replace his real. This killing spree he's on is simply his way of figuring out how best to accomplish the murder without anyone being the wiser. He has no consciousness to appeal to, no soul. He would stab you both just to time how long it took for you to bleed out. I know you've dealt with true evil, but even evil involves logic. What I'm dealing with regarding Monty is pure instinct."

Cheesecake's ears perked up as Sere discussed the

dangers Kendell could be facing. "We're not suggesting picking up guns and searching for your demon," Kendell said. "The real Montgomery Fisher is a CPA in the Quarter. Talking to him about our taxes is hardly a matter of life or death, even though it can feel that way at times."

Sere shook her head in disbelief. "You don't get it. Monty is a projection of Mr. Fisher. I can't risk that this doppelgänger might receive his real's thoughts and experiences. You two meeting the real guy could put you in Monty's line of fire. If he figures out how important you are to me, or that you might know what he's up to, he'll come after you. His prime motivation is replacing Mr. Fisher, and he has no reservations about killing anyone who gets in his way."

"But that's impossible. His face is all over the news. Even if Monty did acquire all of Mr. Fisher's knowledge, he'd have to realize those closest to his real would notice the change."

Sere worked the wig onto her head. It hadn't been much to begin with, but after a day under her helmet, stuffed in her saddlebag, and tossed around the back of a van the thing looked, smelled, and felt like a dead swamp rat. "You keep applying logic to his thought processes. For the last twenty-plus years, his brain has been merely the shadow of Mr. Fisher's thoughts. Now that Monty has escaped hell, his thinking is closer to that of a toddler going after some candy, only in a demonic sense. So instead of throwing a tantrum at not getting what he wants, he goes on a killing spree."

"So what is your plan? Find out how Mr. Fisher lives and

intercept Monty? Then what? Based on what happened to Thomas when you decapitated his doppelgänger, you might be sacrificing one homicidal maniac in the creation of another."

Sere rolled up the pant leg of her jeans and fastened the knife holster to her leg. The blade she'd taken off Thomas, she stashed under her belt below the cotton dress shirt. "Honestly, I don't know what will happen. Thomas's doppelgänger in hell worked for Professor Yates, so he wasn't strictly a copy like Monty. I understand how Monty thinks because I'm used to the same basic thought processes. But in addition to having my own soul that separates me from this projected body, I also have the education you and your friends gave me. I'll outwit him when the time comes, but for now, I just need to know what he's up to. And much as I love you, I need the freedom to conduct my hunt as I see fit. Figuring out answers to your questions is only making me second-guess myself. Lie low, and don't make a big deal of my visit. I'll be in touch once this is over."

"We'll stay out of your way, but you can't honestly believe we're just going to sit on the sidelines."

10

*K*endell had a point about Sere walking through the Quarter, though having someone by her side wasn't likely to help. The bombing that had taken out her father's old bank had happened only a couple of blocks away, coating the whole area in paranormally infected marble dust. Nineteen years later, Sere's skin itched as if it were an animal hide being tanned in some noxious chemical mixture.

"I'm imagining things." Between the heavy rains, city cleanups after drunken festivals, and the occasional hurricane, any dust would have been washed out to the Gulf of Mexico long ago. She increased her pace to a determined walk just the same.

She had precious little to go on in terms of understanding Montgomery Fisher. Each time she'd tried wading through the folder of information, her eyes had glazed over in boredom. How people could spend their days cloistered away behind a desk, staring at numbers, was beyond her. Searching for his office while wandering through the Quarter increased her feeling of claustrophobia. The buildings were too close together, the streets too congested with traffic, the sidewalks much too narrow, and the people—either from prolonged intoxication or simply morning dullness—were completely oblivious to where they were going. In desperation, she ducked into a small bar to escape the maddening throng of people.

"This is the Swamp Strangler's list of suspected victims." The news never seemed to shut up. The bar's version blared from two big screens against opposite walls. Sere felt hemmed in by the stereophonic images, both photographic and hand drawn. When she saw the pencil sketch of her face, she hunched down over the bar, hoping no one would notice. "This woman, originally thought to be an accomplice, has now been added to the list of potential victims. The people of New Orleans are encouraged to stay on guard but under no circumstances to confront the suspected perpetrator of these horrific crimes." A drawing of Monty's face completely filled both screens.

The woman bartender leaned against the counter, shaking her head. "Why some people feel the need to kill indiscriminately is beyond me. What can I get you?"

"Black coffee, as strong as you've got."

"Rough night?" The woman turned her back to Sere and pulled the black-stained half-full glass pot from the coffeemaker.

"Something like that." Sere scratched at her black wig,

wondering how much longer she'd have to endure the dead-rat smell. *It would have been nice if one of you women had taught me something about makeup and hair coloring when I was growing up, though I probably wouldn't have listened. It wasn't like I was trying to impress anyone in hell.* She settled the wig back in position. People focused on pictures of criminals, but the faces of their victims were often forgotten by the next commercial break. However, while the general population looked the other way, the cops would still be on the lookout for the mysterious redheaded woman with the vintage motorcycle.

"Shit." Sere took a deep swig of the bitter brew.

"Can I get you something stronger? Hair of the dog maybe?"

As tempting as it was, alcohol wasn't going to help with her observation of Monty's real. "No, thank you. I just realized I'm supposed to meet someone, and I'm late. You wouldn't happen to know where I could find a CPA named Montgomery Fisher?"

"That's who that guy looks like! I've been wracking my brain trying to figure it out. Mr. Fisher might be a little older and maybe a pound or two heavier, but those two could be brothers if not twins. The only real difference is their eyes. The Swamp Strangler's eyes are as cold and dead as a freezer-burned hamburger. Mr. Fisher's are always smiling, even during tax season."

"So you know him?" Sere pushed the ceramic cup and saucer to the center of the bar.

"Mostly just from seeing him pass on the street. He's helped out a couple of service-worker friends. One of them insisted he join her for a drink. That's the only time I met him. Trust me, though—whatever your financial woes are, he'll get you squared away. When you see him, tell him he looks like the Swamp Strangler. He'll get a kick of out it."

"If you like the guy—in light of all the news attention—it might be better if you kept that as an inside joke." Sere pulled out a five and set it next to the coffee cup. "And where might I find him?"

"Up one block and over two. Keep an eye out for a used bookstore. His office is really easy to miss."

~

DURING THE SHORT WALK, Sere ran through every scenario she could think of for using Mr. Fisher to intercept Monty. Even if she could lie, each story she thought up sounded more outlandish than the last. "I'm just going to tell him the truth, or at least as much of it as he's likely to accept."

She stood in front of the used bookstore, wishing she could while away the day, thumbing through other people's thoughts, instead of dropping a truth bomb on someone who didn't deserve it. Still looking through the smudged window at the display of first editions, she pushed open the door to the CPA's office.

"Can I help you?" The receptionist, with her horn-rimmed glasses and bun of gray hair, looked like she would have been more at home in the store next door. *She probably came with the building.*

"I need to see Mr. Fisher. I'm afraid I don't have an appointment."

The woman lowered her glasses and let them hang from the delicate gold chain around her neck. "Let me see if he's busy." She picked up an ancient push-button phone receiver. From the smile the woman failed to hide, Sere suspected Mr. Fisher spent more time snoozing behind his desk than fixing people's economic nightmares.

The door to the back office opened to display a gentleman wearing a seersucker suit and bow tie. "I don't get many walk-ins. Please come in and have a seat. I'm sure we can untangle whatever situation has you in its grasp."

The bartender was right. Mr. Fisher's eyes displayed a constant state of good humor. He looked as if he were just waiting for someone to tell him a joke so he could bust out laughing.

Sere waited until he'd closed the door and resumed his seat behind the wooden desk. From the computer displays filled with graphs and spreadsheets that occupied the table behind him, she assumed the old-time-accountant image was mostly for show. *You are a sly one, aren't you? Old-fashioned exterior to lure people in and make them comfortable, but as sharp as a tack. I see where Monty is getting his cunning.*

"I'm with the Scratchy Dog night club on Frenchmen Street."

"So this is a business situation?" He sat a little straighter as if normal folk needed a more laid-back money manager and business owners more professionalism.

"No, not really. I didn't want you to think I was just some crazy woman off the street. Kendell Summer and Myles Garrison have helped raise me since I was a little girl."

He sat back in his leather office chair. "I used to love going to see Polly Urethane and the Strippers at the Scratchy Dog when I was just starting out."

"Kendell played guitar with the group."

He looked up at the ceiling with a wistful air of remembrance. "Olympia Stain. That woman could shred a set of strings like no one's business."

"You really were a fan if you knew her real name along with her stage name."

He settled back into position behind the desk and laughed. "I hate to admit it, but I've still got a flyer around here somewhere with all of their signatures on it: Polly, Olympia, Minerva Wax, Scraper, and Lynn Seed. I used to catch them every Friday night. I hope they're not the ones in need of help."

Sere put her hands in her lap, feeling like a little girl called to the principal's office. "They're all fine. My problem —or rather your problem—doesn't involve money. I'm sure you've seen the news stories about the Swamp Strangler."

His eyes lost the crinkles at the sides, indicating a growing seriousness. "I don't pay much attention to the local sensationalist nonsense, but it would be impossible not to know what's going on."

She decided the best course was to just lay it out. "He's coming for you."

Mr. Fisher kept eye contact without blinking for an uncomfortably long time. "This is a joke."

"I wish it were. You must have noticed the physical resemblance. I'm here to stop him."

The CPA shook his head and let out a disbelieving

chuckle. "Lady, if you're running a con, you've picked the wrong mark. I've got two daughters, one at LSU and one applying to Tulane. You can see the office I work in. Other than the computers, it hasn't been updated in a decade. And my wife is intent on remodeling every room of our house. To think that I would have money to extort is just a laugh."

Sere scratched her wig until it came loose. *Fuck it.* Instead of continuing the ruse, she slid the mop of hair off the back of her head, revealing her matted red locks. *Monty has probably already seen through the disguise, and if not, seeing that I'm still after him might hasten his next move. The sooner he comes after this sweet old man, the sooner he ends his killing rampage.* "I'm not asking for anything, and I'm not lying to you. Tell me you haven't noticed the resemblance."

He turned his palms toward the ceiling. "Those crime drawings are like Rorschach tests. People see what they want to see. So sure, my wife ribbed me about being some mass-murdering CPA, but no one would take the similarities seriously. Fluff up your hair a little, and you could pass..."

She let the realization settle in for a moment. "I am the woman in the drawing, but I'm not his victim, and I'm not his accomplice. I've been after him from the beginning."

"So you're some kind of bounty hunter?"

"I suppose that's as accurate a description as any. Though at this point, my adversary and I are more like the snake and the mongoose. If he gets the drop on me, he'll kill me without giving it a second thought."

"What do you want from me? And why on earth would he be after me?"

Sere struggled with how much to tell the sweet old man. "Let me ask you: have you been feeling okay lately?"

He resumed his analytical stare. "Does it show?"

"No. You look fine to me, but this guy has an ability to sap a person's strength." *And not just any person,* she thought, but she didn't want to burden Mr. Fisher with information about the direct connection to his doppelgänger until she had to.

"I'm hardly ever sick. I've got the constitution of an ox. So when I collapsed yesterday morning, my wife demanded I see our doctor. He says I'm fine, and he ran enough tests to know. That didn't do me much good last night, though, when I was flat on my back, struggling to breathe."

Sere felt a combination of panic for Mr. Fisher and excitement that Monty was struggling enough that he had to draw that much energy from his real. *Those shotgun pellets must still be raising hell inside him.* "Have you had any visions you couldn't explain, like you were someone else?"

"Nothing like that, just an exhaustion that drains every cell in my body."

Damn it. I guess I won't be getting a glimpse into what Monty's up to. "He must be closer than I thought."

Mr. Fisher leaned across his desk. "I don't get it. You still haven't explained why he would be after me. I thought all of the Swamp Strangler's victims were the result of random encounters."

"He's learning how to kill without the death being noticed. His plan is to take up your life once you're out of the scene."

The middle-aged gentleman shook his head as if nothing

made any sense. "Even a psychopath would see the impossibility of trying to live someone else's life. He might look a little like me, but he'd never make the illusion stick."

Sere stood up and spread her arms so Mr. Fisher could get a good look at her. "How old do you think I am?"

"Early twenties?"

She smiled at hearing his attempt at chivalry. "You're sweet. Saying I was in my midtwenties would not have been an insult." She turned her back on him and focused on Jennifer Ellen Cranston—then Jennifer Ellen Williams—as a teenaged cheerleader.

When she turned back around, she could see the shock in Mr. Fisher's eyes. "What the hell? Can you teach me that trick? I could make you a lot of money—"

"It's not a trick," she blurted. Her voice was at a higher, more youthful pitch. Her clothes felt even baggier than when she'd put them on. "The guy that's after you can do the same thing. He can look exactly like you if he wants." The sound of her own voice was beginning to bug her. She could just envision Jennifer, the popular girl, flirting with all the high school boys. She turned back toward the door and let her self-image return to that of the woman she'd worked so hard at creating.

Mr. Fisher continued talking, as if Sere had slipped behind a dressing screen to change and he didn't want to make a big deal of her exposure. "I've lived my whole life in New Orleans, so I've seen some stuff I never could explain. But I still don't get one thing. Why would anyone want *my* life? Don't get me wrong. I love my family, and I've worked hard to build this business, but

I've got college tuitions to deal with, a rapidly approaching retirement that scares the hell out of me, people who rely on my expert advice—stresses a middle-aged man would want to escape, not kill to acquire."

She felt better at her proper size and age. "Why does anyone fixate on anything? He is a psychopath."

"What happens if he succeeds?" From the worried look in his eyes, Sere suspected the man was more concerned with his family than his personal safety.

"You mean after he kills you and assumes your life? I don't know. I doubt his end game is to work his remaining years as a CPA and retire to a life of ease while watching his daughters achieve lives of their own. Your history would give him a safe cover identity for whatever future crimes he has in mind." *Though I doubt this demon has planned that far ahead,* Sere thought.

"What makes you think you can stop him?" Mr. Fisher asked.

Though she wanted to trust the kindly CPA, she couldn't risk Monty listening in on everything that might be said. Unlike her disgusted avoidance of Jennifer, Monty was probably doing all he could to hear every one of Mr. Fisher's thoughts in his attempt at intercepting and killing the man. She needed to keep the information to what Monty would figure out on his own.

"Up until now, his attacks have been random. That's been an advantage for him. I'm not sure you're next, but from what I've seen, he's perfected his technique enough to make a try at you. For the first time, that puts me one step ahead of him. I've been playing catchup since the beginning, and that's a bad position to be in."

"What would you have me do—run and hide?"

She pointed at a stack of blank paper. "Write down your week's activities, including times and addresses. The more I know about you, the better I can protect you."

~

SERE LEFT the office with the neatly graphed page of Mr. Fisher's activities folded up in her pocket and headed down toward the river. With the CPA on a predictable path and the people Sere cared about on the sidelines, she almost felt as if she had control of the situation. She didn't need Joe's edicts, however, to know the fallacy of such an instinct. People often thought they had the upper hand right up until the moment the knife went into their hearts.

The logical move—and the one she'd carefully laid out for Monty to assume—would be for her to hide in every available bush and spy on Mr. Fisher like some love-struck stalker. So long as Monty thought that was what she was doing, he'd be lying low, trying to find her before she ambushed him—a situation that would keep Mr. Fisher safe for the time being. However, it wasn't a ruse that was likely to last long. Even with Monty operating on little more than a reptilian brain, he'd eventually figure out there wasn't a threat lurking in the shadows. *His second-guessing still puts me one step ahead. What I told Mr. Fisher wasn't a lie.*

The real tidbit of information was Mr. Fisher's illness. Sere could draw on Jennifer if the need were great enough, but the emotional energy required to create the direct bond without the enhancement of Professor Yates's equipment was like getting lost in an intense, prolonged orgasm—potentially addictive and psychically draining. If Monty was relying on that connection to his real, something had to be wrong. As Mr. Fisher's illness was recent, Sere hoped Monty's malady was more than just the buckshot. Whatever was causing Monty to draw on Mr. Fisher, he was behaving like a wounded animal. That made him vulnerable but also potentially more dangerous.

The breeze off the water invigorated Sere's skin as she headed toward the professor's lab. She needed her equipment if she was going back on the hunt. Playing the undercover female sleuth hadn't come naturally. She was a woman of action, not conversation. The disguise had worked well enough. No cop had stopped her to question the resemblance to the drawing plastered on yesterday's newscast, and Auntie Kendell and Uncle Myles hadn't been burdened with the image of Sere as a badass motorcycle-riding demon hunter—though having to rescue her from a knife-wielding psycho probably wasn't much better.

Sere stopped for a moment and squeezed her eyes shut. *When they found me, I was the one with the blades. Same difference.* She continued on. Every step put her closer to being out of the couple's idea of street clothes and back in her riding leathers complete with shotgun. Though she'd only had the weapon with her for a short time, there was a reassurance at having the weight strapped to her back. Even if she wasn't much good at pulling the trigger, the section of pipe and solid wood made for an impressive bludgeon.

She was still considering how much of the undercover city image she could shed when she opened the door to Professor Yates's offices. The man was wildly disorganized, but the smashed equipment, disgorged file folders, and busted interior windows were enough evidence that his latest encounter had been more adversarial than collaborative.

"Professor Yates?" she called out, not really expecting an answer.

"He's getting away out the back door, and he's got your gun." The old man gasped out the words.

Not this time. Sere pulled out the switchblade she'd taken off Thomas and raced down the hallway. The back door was just settling closed as she turned sideways and used her shoulder on it like a battering ram. Back out in the bright light of day, she could see that Monty had a good twenty-yard head start. She flipped open the blade, twisted her body, and launched the dagger with all of the momentum she could muster. It penetrated the left side of his back.

"Fuck you, Monty!" she yelled. He didn't even slow down.

She still had her knife, but as it was stashed under the pant leg of her jeans, she would need to stop running to fish out the blade. With her gun in his hand, Monty was sprinting like a relay runner headed toward the finish line. She stood with fists clenched and watched him bolt onto the back of a passing streetcar.

Facts swirled around her like a swarm of annoying gnats. She'd landed a knife wound. That meant Monty was in worse shape and would be pulling harder against Mr.

Fisher. But he had her gun, and that meant the shells could just as easily disrupt her connection to her real as his. *Professor Yates...*

"Shit!" She turned away from the retreating red streetcar and ran back into the building before the pneumatic dampener had a chance to shut the door. She fell to her knees beside the gangly gentleman gasping for air on the floor. Blood was oozing out of scattered holes in his chest. She put her hands over the wounds, unsure of what else to do. "Stay with me. I can't lose you too."

"He was far enough away that the pellets couldn't penetrate very deep," Professor Yates gasped. "Get me my phone so I can call for help."

She kept her hand over the bloody holes while scanning his desk. "Got it."

"See if you can find something to stop this bleeding."

"Is that your polite way of reminding me your phone won't work with me standing here? I'll try the bathroom." Blood again streamed out of his body when she took her hand away. She ran to the space that was as much a utility closet as a bathroom and pulled open every cabinet, searching for something to stem the rivers of blood escaping from the professor's body.

She could hear his side of the conversation in the next room. "I've been shot. Bring the emergency kit. Don't tell Kendell or Myles. Just get here quickly. Sere's safe."

As soon as she heard the phone land back on the desk, she rushed in with an armload of towels and rolls of duct tape. "Who did you call?"

"Polly. She's been helping me out practically since the

day we set up the virtual-reality overlay in your father's hell."

"You could have called the paramedics. That would have been safer." She helped him to sit up against the side of the desk so she could wrap the terrycloth around his chest.

"Bullshit. You can't be discovered. For the last two decades, this lab's primary function has been to keep you whole. The medics would bring the cops, and they ask too many questions."

She needed to keep him from going into shock. Though the pellets hadn't punctured his lungs, he had lost a lot of blood. However, she also had a lot of questions and not a lot of time. "What did Monty want? And how the hell did he get past your security system?"

"He wants to be free of his real." Professor Yates looked up at her with glazed eyes. "He's not doing well. A person on the street wouldn't notice anything unusual, but my computer monitoring system sees doppelgängers as they are, not as they appear."

"I don't understand."

He pointed at the laptop that lay on its side across the room. "Boot that up, and open the most recent file."

She pulled the tape tight across his chest. The once grungy-white towels were quickly turning dark red. He held the makeshift bandage in place while she crawled over to the computer and poked at the keys. *So long as you don't have an external connection, there's no reason for you not to obey me.* A video started playing of a man walking up to the front door of the receptionist's office. When he looked up at the camera, Sere figured out what the professor had meant. "He doesn't look like he has any skin."

"Exactly." The professor coughed hard but didn't spit out any blood. "He must still have those rock pellets in him. Not that he'd be doing much better even if he hadn't been shot. The longer he's out of hell, the less complete his projection. His internal organs will all continue to function, but superficial aspects like skin and hair pigment will slowly fade. So far, only you and my equipment can detect the change, but eventually, others will notice too. And with those stones in him, the difference in his appearance will happen sooner rather than later."

Sere enhanced the image. Muscles, veins, teeth, and eyes all looked unnaturally prominent. Only a light sheen of milky-white skin covered the surface. "He barely looks human. And you say I'll be able to see this with my naked eyes?"

"You're from the same dimension, so yes. People in this realm vary in their perceptions of reality. The more empathetic people are, the sooner they will notice the truth. As for my sensors, I don't know why they didn't alert me. Figuring out what went wrong will be my first chore once Polly gets me back on my feet."

"And what about Montgomery Fisher?"

Professor Yates pointed at the screen. "He'll see exactly what you see."

Great. I drove the poor man to the brink of insanity, and now Monty is going to push him over the edge. She kept the knowledge to herself. The professor already had enough to deal with, being shot and all.

Polly rushed in the front door, carrying an overstuffed backpack. She pushed past Sere as if she weren't even there and dropped the pack next to the professor. "What happened?"

"He got hold of Sere's gun and shot me with that paranormal buckshot."

Polly started pulling out equipment and medical supplies from the bag. "Good thing he shot you and not Sere." She held up what looked like a steampunk electromagnet. "Do you think this thing will work on you?"

"It should. The energy it'll pull won't be mine but the pellets'. If anything, it should work better since my body is actively trying to reject the alternate-dimension foreign objects."

Polly tossed Sere the end of the wire. "Plug that into a wall socket."

Nice to see you too. The lack of a greeting on their first meeting in the same dimension, however, only increased Sere's impression of the fortysomething band manager as a no-nonsense, as-hard-as-nails leader who could seemingly make things happen by sheer force of will.

She stuck the plug in the socket. "Good to go."

The wand in Polly's hand made zapping and popping sounds that didn't sound safe. She lowered the flat end over the bloodstained towels and started running it like an iron over the surface.

"Damn," the professor said. "Remind me to add a cooling coil to that thing. It feels like lightning bolts are being extracted from my flesh."

"Hush up, old man," Polly said. "This only takes care of

the paranormal part of your injuries. You've still lost a lot of blood. You need to take it easy until we can get you to the hospital."

"Yes, ma'am." He settled back against the desk.

Polly ran the device over his chest and sides three times until she was satisfied the magnet had finished its work. "Help me unwrap him. With any luck, the pellets will be nestled in the fabric of the towels. They may be a little hot, so watch where you touch."

"Right." The duct tape Sere had so hastily wrapped around the towels combined with the professor's blood to make for a sticky, gooey mess to remove. As Sere took off the saturated rags, Polly grabbed boxes of gauze and bandages from the bag.

"Once we get this bleeding under control, get your things, and hightail it out of here. I'll have Kendell bring the band's bus and drive us to the ER. We'll say the professor had an experiment go sideways, creating an explosion. We can't risk the authorities showing up here and somehow making a connection between this lab and the Swamp Strangler."

Sere made a mental inventory of everything she'd left behind. "I understand. You take care of your own."

Polly turned on her with an animal ferocity. "You're included in that family. If the cops start messing with this equipment, you're the one who will be in the most danger. I'm only being abrupt with you because I know you can take it."

Sere swallowed hard. "I'm sorry. I should have realized."

"Go easy on the girl, Pol," Professor Yates said. "You can't expect her to understand every human interaction."

"Before I go," Sere said, "I need to know what Monty wanted, what he took, and what I'm up against."

Professor Yates struggled to sit upright against the desk. "He came in the back door like Frankenstein's monster, smashing equipment and demanding answers about his existence. He grabbed your gun and started aiming it around the room like he wanted to burn this whole place down but didn't know where to start. Along with losing skin pigment, he's apparently also losing nerve endings. Pain didn't seem to register at all."

"That would explain why the knife I buried in his back didn't slow him down," Sere said.

"He'll feel it later once the adrenaline wears off," the professor said. "His brain can only process so many stimulations at once—rage being his current dominant expression. I tried reasoning with him the way I would with a toddler throwing a tantrum, but in spite of his questions, he clearly wasn't looking for answers."

"I talked with Joe about Monty's possible motivations. We came to the conclusion he wants to kill his real and take over that life. If he's losing what little mental capacity he had, however, I'm beginning to wonder if that's still his intention."

"I doubt intention has anything to do with it at this point. If you hadn't busted in, I have no doubt he would have killed me and torched this lab. He sees everyone else walking around independent of my equipment and figures he should be able to as well."

Polly double-checked her work in stopping the bleeding. "Wouldn't that just destroy him, though?"

"He doesn't see us as providing for his existence." Professor Yates nodded toward his equipment. "To him, this is more like the electronic walls of his hell prison. Now that he's escaped the physical realm, he believes his continued suffering is the result of our efforts and his real."

Sere had hoped there was some part of Monty she could reason with, but more and more, it seemed he really was just a dangerous bug to be squashed. And the damn demonic cockroach was getting away. "Is there any other way to safely destroy him other than the marble shotgun pellets? Because they don't seem to be as effective as I'd like."

"We don't have time for this shit," Polly said. "I need to get the professor to the hospital. I love you, Sere. Now, for your own good, get the hell out of here, and don't look back."

Polly was right. The longer it took for Sere to gather the pieces of the puzzle, the longer the professor would have to suffer. It seemed every person she came in contact with, she put in danger. As desperate as she was to get changed, getting out of the lab had to be her first priority. She headed to the back room, where she'd seen her belongings and where Monty had stolen her single-barreled shotgun.

Her snakes hissed and rattled when she threw her saddlebags over her shoulder. "I missed you guys too." She scooped up the backpack filled with shotgun shells that lay open on its side. There was no way to know how many boxes Monty had absconded with, but he clearly had more shells than just what she'd left loaded in the gun. Her bedroll still had an inner firmness, indicating she at least still had the four-barreled blaster.

"I suppose I should be happy we're now equally armed, but honor be damned. I'd just as soon shoot the son of a bitch in the back and be done with it. Honorable confrontations only extend to adversaries with souls. I wouldn't build a human-sized robot just so some mosquito could crawl in and face me on equal terms."

Her snakes rattled their objection.

"Higher-functioning animals have souls. Insects do not. Monty is nothing more than a hell cockroach with a gun. I'll stomp him out the first opportunity I get."

Satisfied that she'd gathered up everything that might connect Professor Yates to her—and thereby to the Swamp Strangler—Sere hopped on the Triton and walked it to the back door. Before heading out, she yelled over her shoulder, "See you both when this is over. I'm trusting you to take care of those we love, Polly."

"Ride hard and ride fast, girl."

11

*S*ere kick-started the Triton. Time was against her. Again, she was riding into battle without being properly outfitted for what was to come. The loose jeans and flappy cotton shirt weren't ideal riding attire, and they'd be even more of a hindrance when it came to a fight. Her boots were still in her bags with the snakes, which meant her knife was strapped to her leg—not exactly easily accessible. Monty, however, wouldn't be just sitting around, waiting for her to get changed.

Not that he was in optimum fighting condition, either. Between the rock pellets and separation from hell, his translucency was going to make it impossible for him to step into Mr. Fisher's life. His plan had been doomed from the start, but now even he had to see the futility of it. With the new knife wound to contend with, Monty would be sucking on Mr. Fisher's life force like a college kid on spring break draining a cheap daiquiri. Sere had to assume the doppelgänger would still have his sights set on killing the old man, but his intentions would be based on pure anger and frustration with no possibility of real victory. As a cornered, wounded animal with nothing to lose and hopped up on human energy, Monty would be more dangerous than ever.

Sere took a hard left under the freeway overpass onto Saint Charles Avenue. From the itinerary Mr. Fisher had provided, the CPA should be home for lunch. She swerved between cars, potholes, and pedestrians, wondering if Monty would confront the man at home or wait outside until he left for work. Either way, the murderer was once again a step ahead.

To avoid the infuriating obstacles, she leaned over the gas tank, shifted the bike up a gear, and jumped the tires onto a rail of the streetcar line. Like a woman running on a tightrope, she trusted her instincts to keep her balanced as she flew past screaming people and honking horns. At Bordeaux Street, she hopped off the track and turned toward the river.

I just hope I didn't spend too much time dealing with Professor Yates. Polly was right. I didn't have time for such bullshit. I should have just grabbed my bike and torn off after Monty. But had she done that, the professor would likely have succumbed to his wounds before being able to reach his phone. Plus, Monty had her gun. She would have been an easy target following along behind the streetcar.

Second-guessing herself was becoming a bad habit and one of no practical use while she was in pursuit of a mass murderer. She stopped under the limbs of a live oak that covered the street a block from Mr. Fisher's house and consulted the CPA's schedule. *Drive home for lunch at 12:15. I own a 2013 black Jeep Cherokee.* Her analog wristwatch read 12:25. From where she stood, she could see there wasn't a car in his driveway. As a man of precision, Mr. Fisher was mostly likely never late for anything. She eased the Triton from its hiding spot and drove down the street at a moderate speed, hoping not to attract attention.

She stopped cold at the base of the driveway. *Fuck. I wonder what the chances are that Mr. Fisher is an aficionado of Ducati Monsters.* Sitting alongside the Queen Anne Victorian sat the familiar black bike she'd hoped to never see again. "I suppose there's no point in hiding now."

She pulled the four-barreled shotgun out of her bedroll under the headlight of her bike. Looking like a door-to-door mercenary for hire, she approached the house. "You in there, Bart?"

The rugged bartender opened the door. "Mr. Fisher is in trouble. His wife is worried sick."

"That much, I could figure out on my own. What are *you* doing here?"

He stepped out of the entrance and closed the door. "Joe thought you could use backup. I was performing a basic pincer move. With you working your way up from New Orleans and me chasing Monty south, I had hoped we could trap him. Too bad you were late."

Sere considered slapping some sense into the muscular dude. "*Your* plan. Not mine. And it only would have worked if you'd bothered telling me about it."

"I'm not standing here arguing with you, especially while

you're swinging that scatter gun. If I'd told you my idea, you just would have objected and probably done something foolish to foil my attempt to help. Going up against an enemy alone when you don't have to is just stupid."

"So now you're calling me stupid?" She was having trouble controlling the volume of her voice. "Who's the one standing on the porch with his dick in his hand?"

He checked the door behind him. "Are we going to argue, or do you want to go find this asshole before he kills your accountant?"

Sere tensed up, ready for battle. "You know where they went?"

"When the Jeep sped past me with the masked man in the passenger seat aiming a gun at Mr. Fisher behind the wheel, I rushed up to the house to find out what happened. Mrs. Fisher was desperate for any help. They were quietly having lunch, discussing how they were going to pay for their youngest daughter's tuition, when the madman burst in, wielding the shotgun, and forced Mr. Fisher out the door." Bart held up a cell phone. From the picture of puppies on the screensaver, Sere guessed it wasn't his. "Mrs. Fisher keeps a tracker on her phone for all their cars in case one gets stolen."

Peachy. So to find him, I'm at your mercy. Weakness wasn't something to confess while on the hunt. She took a deep, calming breath. "I suppose it was Joe who told you the Swamp Strangler was after Mr. Fisher."

"He was just trying to help. You were pretty emotional when I left you at Riley's, so I made the run down to Joe's cabin to make sure I hadn't made a huge mistake letting you take off on your own. We both thought you could use someone covering your ass."

"And you of course appointed yourself as head ass watcher."

He hustled down the walkway toward the motorcycles. "This isn't just about you. Stories of serial killers coming out of the swamps have a way of cutting into my business. People don't go drinking at night if they think someone with a knife is lurking in the shadows."

"So you figured you'd just sit in the bushes, whacking off and watching while I did battle? You could have stopped the asshole before he ever entered the house."

He threw his leg over the crotch rocket and lifted his helmet from the handlebars. "If you had let me explain rather than fighting with me, we'd already be on the road. I couldn't exactly tail the psycho through the swamps, but I figured eventually he'd show up here at the Fisher house. The real question is, where the hell were you? When I saw the murderer sneaking up the street, I figured you had to be slinking through the bushes after him or hiding in the attic for the ambush. I lay back so I wouldn't get caught in your crossfire. I only took matters into my own hands when they tore off down the street with you nowhere to be seen."

Sere gripped the butt of her shotgun. "Was that a cut about my marksmanship?"

He cranked over the Ducati's engine. "I was only trying to let you play out whatever plan you were running. I guessed if you weren't following the murderer, maybe you were hiding in Mr. Fisher's vehicle. But you're not running a plan, are you?"

She couldn't admit that he was right. "We're wasting time. I suppose I'll have to follow you."

~

SERE WAS STEAMING mad as she followed Bart's Ducati, but she knew her irritation at him was only a transference of her self-condemnation. She'd wasted too much time with Kendell and Myles. Had she not taken the familial detour, she wouldn't have been stabbed by Thomas and lost a whole night to being looked after like a sick child. If she'd stayed focused, she could have been ahead of Bart at figuring out the obvious ploy of lying in wait at the Fisher residence. Even if Monty had found her, the battle would have been between her and him the way it should have been. Hell, if she'd just bolted the moment Polly showed up to take care of the professor, she still might have been able to track Monty the way Bart had assumed she would.

"How the hell am I supposed to know this stuff? Joe taught me to defend myself and work alone, not coordinate my activities like I belonged to a pack of wolves." She'd never wanted to stop off at a bar for a shot and a fight more than she did right then.

When they reached the freeway on-ramp, the Ducati shot ahead as if Bart had fed nitrous into the carburetor. Giving chase redirected Sere's thoughts from what she should have done to what she needed to do. Monty was headed over the Crescent City Connection toward the Jean Lafitte swamp. *Makes sense. Monty would be looking for somewhere to dispose of the body, but he needs Mr. Fisher to do the driving.* Monty had to believe he'd given Sere the slip if he was headed to an area she understood so well. Being in cities—with their crowded streets, confining buildings, and lack of vegetation to provide cover—meant she'd had to play a role that didn't come naturally. Once out in the marshes and rivers, she could slip through the water and plants like a snake slithering after its prey.

She patted her saddlebag, knowing how much her serpents would enjoy being back in their natural habitat. He was still a step ahead, but he'd misjudged her determination, and—as much as she hated to admit it—Bart's cleverness. "That hunky fool still should have minded his own business," she grumbled.

Sere leaned low over her handlebars to cut down on wind resistance as Bart cut through the freeway traffic. Though the Ducati was more powerful, it was burdened with a bulky rider who relied more on brawn—or in this case horsepower—than smarts. She didn't have any problems keeping up. When he finally took the off-ramp, however, he didn't even bother to downshift. "That idiot is going to get us both killed before we even reach the swamp."

Weaving around the city traffic gave Sere the clear advantage. Bart could only shoot through gaps wide enough to accommodate his beefy arms and shoulders. At the high speeds he was maintaining, he needed to steer a predictable path. She kept her front tire glued to his tail like a quarterback following a linebacker through the opponent's defensive line.

When they transitioned from well-maintained city

streets to rugged gravel roads winding through dense marshes, Bart finally reduced his speed to a sane pace. Sere checked her watch. *Fifteen minutes from front door to bayou's edge. That must be some kind of record.*

He pulled into a wide turnout and shut down his engine. When he took off his helmet, she wondered how he managed to remove it from his ego-inflated head. "I suppose you think that was clever," she said, "nearly getting us both killed. Or was that payback for our first ride together where I lost you in my dust?"

He nodded down the road. "The Jeep is just around that corner. It only arrived a couple of minutes before us. I thought it might be nice if we showed up *before* Mr. Fisher was killed instead of after."

She choked as much on having to admit he was right as on the road dust she'd been swallowing. "What weapons did you bring?"

He swung his muscular leg off the back of his bike. The first knife he pulled from his hip and set on the seat of his Ducati looked like some adolescent boy's idea of a cool weapon. "Cold Steel Natchez Bowie knife. This thing will cut through damn near anything, but I hardly ever have to use it. One look at the massive blade, and whoever I'm facing backs down." The next knife was more her style. "Flat black Ontario MK 3 Navy knife. It's an inch shorter than your Fairbairn-Sykes, making it easier to wield in tight combat."

"I'll bet that's the excuse you give all the girls." Sere couldn't resist the jibe. His cold stare made it clear he didn't find the reference to his manhood humorous. *Muscular military types and reptiles—exactly the same lack of a sense of humor.*

"If that's about the size of my cock, I'll have you know I'm quite well endowed."

"I guess I'll just have to take your word on that for the time being. What other dangerous weapons are you packing?"

He pulled what looked like an updated mercenary version of a Swiss Army knife out of his boot. "GIGN Glauca B1, developed for France's counterterrorist unit. I've MacGyvered my way out of countless situations with this baby. That's it for the knives." He reached around to the small of his back. "I also carry this Smith & Wesson snub nose .38. It's not pretty, but as a bartender, I've found that knives aren't always the ultimate solution to drunken brawls." He nodded at her boot. "I've shown you mine. Time to fess up with what you've got."

She pulled her trusty knife from her boot. "You already know about this one. I used to carry a sawed-off single-barrel shotgun on my back, but Monty stole it from my supplies." She reached under her headlight and pulled the four-barreled blaster from her bedroll. "This is what will ultimately kill Monty. The shells are custom designed for his special vulnerabilities."

"You travel light, but then, I've seen you fight."

She turned the shotgun around and aimed the butt of the gun toward Bart. "Take it. When the time is right, pepper Monty with as much buckshot as you can blast into him."

Bart had the standard confused, dumb expression she'd

come to expect as he accepted the weapon. "You don't want to do the deed yourself?"

She pointed at the seat of his bike. "Give me your Navy knife. Monty is sure to expect some sort of frontal assault. Most of the paths through the swamps are narrow, circuitous routes without any other way in or out." She unbuttoned her cotton shirt and tossed it onto the seat of her Triton. "What he won't expect is a water assault." She gave Bart a suspicious stare. "Since you're Navy, I would have thought you'd have already guessed my plan." She kicked off her sneakers and unzipped her jeans then added them to the pile. "I'll slip around the small island and approach from the back while you do your best not be noticed coming in from the front."

He handled the shotgun as if he'd just been handed a trophy for second place. "I'm the Navy SEAL. I'm the one who should be making the water approach."

In only her panties, bra, and the knife strapped to her leg, she opened her saddlebags and let the two canebrake rattlers slither up her arms. "Tell you what: take one of these snakes from my arms, and I'll let you make the manly gesture of shedding your clothes and slipping into the reptile-infested waters."

He set the barrel of the gun over his shoulder. "Point taken. This thing looks pretty indiscriminate in what it'll hit. How do you want to coordinate the attack so you're not the one being filled with buckshot?"

Good question. Admitting that she was as susceptible to the custom pellets as Monty, however, would mean divulging more information than she wanted Bart to know.

"Get as close to them as you can, and find a good hiding spot. There's plenty of thick brush, so it shouldn't be a problem. Monty will be looking for someplace along the shore. He won't do anything until he's sure there's an alligator in the vicinity to devour the body, so we have a few minutes at least. Have the gun ready. Wait until he's searching the water, then when I signal you, make enough noise to distract him. Once he turns his back on me, I'll be the one to lunge out of the water—instead of a gator. With the knives, I should be able to calm him down. I need answers before we kill him."

"So I'm just your fallback? You could deal with him easily enough with those blades."

Sere took his Navy knife from the seat of the Ducati. Holding out her arm, she slit her wrist the way she had as a seven-year-old girl. Blood oozed from the wound but quickly coagulated. By the time she'd wiped the blade off on the seat, the slash had almost disappeared. "I heal quickly. So does Monty. I can kill him with the knives, but it won't be easy. Even from a distance, though, that buckshot isn't something his body can tolerate."

Bart picked up the rest of his weapons and stashed them back around his body. "Are you two related?"

"We don't have time for family genealogy. Just be ready when I come up out of the water. I'll tell you when to shoot."

"Don't leave me holding my dick again. If it looks like he's about to kill Mr. Fisher, I'm not going to hesitate."

~

SERE WAITED until Bart was halfway down the road before snagging a couple of shotgun shells from her saddlebag and securing them in the waistband of her underwear. "Time to call in some reinforcements." She stepped gingerly through the vines and tree roots to the water's edge. Spreading out her arms on top of the water, she aimed her snakes toward the welcoming bayou. "Go find Lefty. One way or another, there's going to be a body to dispose of, and I can't trust these overfed, practically domesticated tour-group swamp puppies to know how to devour fresh meat." The two snakes shot off like lightning bolts discharged underwater. Only the slight ripples on the surface of the calm river betrayed their passage.

Sere checked that her knife was securely strapped to her leg. She then took Bart's thick blade and clamped it between her teeth. *Let's see how useful you real creatures are compared to the hell beasts I know.* She crushed one of the shotgun shells in her hand and flung the pebbles out into the water. When she dove into the murky depths, teeming schools of catfish and river gars were waiting for her. Like personal underwater propulsion jets, they swam so close to her that they pulled her along through the interconnected rivers. They didn't leave her until the water became so dense with vegetation that their undulating bodies might be noticed above. When they disbanded, she crept along through the stalks until she couldn't see any light above through the thick mat of water lilies that clung to the shoreline.

Without disturbing the surrounding plants, she lifted her head under a large leaf, feeling like a combination of the little mermaid and a Navy SEAL. *I'd like to have seen Bart do better,* she thought, more pleased with herself than was strictly warranted. The river creatures, after all, were her allies, not her subjects.

Monty screamed at the large pond of open water beyond Sere's aquatic garden. "Where are you goddamned gators? Show yourselves!"

But the surface of the water remained as smooth as glass. She lowered her head back underwater and edged closer to the shore. Her fish companions had swum her out so quickly that she wondered if she had gotten to the island before Bart. She didn't dare make a move until he was in position, but she couldn't wait around all day. Monty's patience wasn't likely to last long. When her eyes again broke the surface, she was staring at the demon's business loafers. Behind him on the ground, Mr. Fisher cowered before the version of himself so hell tortured as to have become nearly unrecognizable.

A slight breeze rustled the leaves of the oak saplings beyond the shore. One of the young trees bent down farther than warranted by the breath of air. Bart flashed the *okay* sign with his fingers, indicating he was in position. *How the hell did he see me? I guess his training is better than I suspected.* When she gave him the return thumbs-up, he rustled the small bush enough to attract Monty's attention.

"What's back there? Have I finally found an alligator? Come on out and face hell."

While Monty was turned away from her, Sere reached out from the swamp, grabbed him by the ankles, and yanked him hard off his feet and halfway into the water. She was on top of him before he had a chance to roll over. With her thin bladed knife, she jabbed him through the back as if pinning him to the shore. She had Bart's Navy knife against his throat before he'd gathered his wits enough to cry out. "We're going to get up out of this water nice and slow."

Monty struggled under her weight. "If you're going to kill me, do it. I'll just regenerate in hell and try again. You don't have anything to threaten me with."

She leaned back and pulled him to his knees with the knife at his carotid artery. "Brave words, but we both know they're a lie. Even if you do come back, you will have forgotten what you apparently learned. Get up." By driving the thin knife up toward his lung, she forced him to rise as if operating him via remote control.

"You're just going to kill me no matter what I say."

"You're not wrong, but I want some answers before I dispatch you back to where you belong. How did you escape hell?"

He continued to move under her knife-edges as if trying to discover a weakness in her hold. "Why should I tell you anything?"

She pulled the black knife tighter to his neck and whispered in his ear so that neither Bart nor Mr. Fisher could hear. "I still have powerful allies in hell. You think you had it bad before? Wait until the entire dimension turns against you."

"I have my allies too."

From the ground, Mr. Fisher let out a bloodcurdling scream and spasmed so hard it looked as if his life was being sucked out of every muscle and organ of his body. Monty used the distraction and increased energy to spin so hard to his left that Sere felt her knife slice through muscle in his neck as he escaped her death threat. Though he had avoided losing his head to Bart's blade, she held tightly to the remaining handle in his back as the razor-sharp steel severed his spinal cord.

He crumpled to the grass, taking the thin blade with him. Sere spun around like a ninja ballerina, building momentum. As she sliced down toward her victim's neck with Bart's Navy knife, Monty rolled his torso over and lifted the barrel of the shotgun from the ground. The satisfying resistance of sharpened metal cutting through tissue and bone was countered by small pellets of paranormal stone penetrating her side. Monty's head rolled off his shoulders and hit the ground while his body remained sitting, propped up with the butt of the shotgun.

"Shoot him!"

Bart ran out from the tree line, shotgun in hand. "Why? He's already dead. He can't hurt you now that he's decapitated."

"Stop arguing logic with me, and fire the goddamned gun." She looked over at Mr. Fisher, fearful she would see the man transform into the demon she'd just dispatched.

Bart came around beside her before leveling the gun at the propped up body. The blast knocked Monty's broken and lifeless torso three feet before it came to rest next to his head.

THE SIDE of Sere's rib cage burned as if hot coals had been

seared into her flesh. She gasped for air. She'd been hurt enough times to know the drill. When she was younger, her body often needed a few minutes to adjust to its new condition. Through rigorous training, she'd cut that time down to seconds. But with each passing moment, Sere felt her grip on her consciousness slipping away. Unfortunately, it wasn't toward a comatose state.

Sere clung to her personal messed-up history while her body sought out any source of energy it could find to combat the disruptive damage the pellets were creating. Her perception glazed over as if she were being put into a nesting doll. *Not fucking Jennifer Cranston again. Please, woman, be doing something other than shopping with that dimwit friend of yours.* But instead of slipping into her real's world, Sere witnessed her body falling into Bart's arms like some movie scene featuring a dumb-ass damsel in distress fainting into her lover's embrace.

"Now we'll face off on my home turf." The man's words were more felt than heard.

She was having trouble breathing. Dirt and grass filled her mouth. The scene of her body in Bart's arms continued to play out in front of her. "Damn it to hell! I must be in Mr. Fisher. He would have been the easiest body to access since his image is being projected into hell."

"Very good." Even without changing her focus, she knew it was Monty standing over her like some egotistical misogynist boyfriend.

"How did you manage the leap?"

"Your boyfriend over there was a little slow with the shotgun, for one. But that wasn't your real mistake."

"I had him shoot the goddamned body." Sere could kick herself for her stupidity.

"Did no one ever bother to tell you only a head shot would kill a zombie?"

"Fucking Artie Andy and his lack of instructions. I'll bet anything he knew and didn't tell me." Being trapped in Mr. Fisher's soul meant every thought came out for Monty to hear.

"Leave her alone." The words shook Sere to her core. Monty fell to the ground and raised his hands over his head as if God himself had spoken.

Sere instantly recognized the voice. "I promise you, Montgomery Fisher, that I will do all I can to get this pestilence out of you."

The intense pain of the buckshot in her side had gotten so much worse that she returned to her body. Someone was pressing a hand hard against her side.

"What the hell?" she said.

"Just once, would you please shut up and let me help you?" The rugged features of Bartender Smooth came into focus. "Tell me what I need to do to keep you from fading out again."

"You have to get the buckshot out of me."

He lifted his hands off her naked torso. Blood started pumping out of her.

"You'll bleed out long before I can get all those pellets removed," Bart said. "Let me wrap you up and get you to the hospital."

His denseness provided a useful distraction to her need for human energy. "We already went through this the last time I was shot. No fucking hospitals. Everyone I know is too far away to help. You're a Navy SEAL. Surely, you must have some medic skills."

"I don't have any supplies, not even a bottle of whiskey to numb you and disinfect the area. Anything I do would hurt like hell and send you into shock."

She reached up and grabbed him by the shirt. "Get these fucking pellets out of me. The pain will keep me focused. You've already seen how fast I can heal." She rolled to her side so the holes would be more accessible and turned her attention to Jennifer. If she did slip into another soul, at least it wouldn't be one plagued by a demon.

Bart yanked off his leather jacket and pressed it to her side. "Push this as hard against the wounds as you can stand to slow down the blood loss. I need to find something to get at those pellets." Bart left her and hunted around the reeds along the swamp until he found a grove of young bamboo. He started hacking at the brown stalks with his MacGyver knife and blew through each one.

Sere looked back at Mr. Fisher. The poor man's eyes had glazed over like he was in a trance. *What the hell am I going to do with you?*

◈

PAIN from the knives and sharpened bamboo skewers that Bart used like straws or chopsticks—depending on the pellet's depth in her flesh—kept Sere from slipping into another person. However, the connection that she'd previously experienced as a hardwired direct link to

Jennifer now felt like blaring, overlapping radio signals— and the paranormal pellets were spinning the dial. Every person in a ten-mile radius seemed to be projecting his or her consciousness for Sere to tap into. If she focused too long on any specific input, she could easily take on that person's identity. Only by remembering the young child that she'd been and her odd upbringing by the handful of people who truly cared about her was she able to maintain some sense of her own identity.

Bart used his GIGN Glauca B1 knife to cut and strip some vines. Then he pulled off his shirt, revealing a muscular, well-tanned chest that perfectly matched his rippling arms. He tenderly pressed the sweat-stained folded cotton to her wounds and secured it in place with the vines. His smell was nearly as intoxicating as the adrenaline she'd relied on to stay sane.

"I think that's it," Bart said.

I'm out here with fucking Tarzan MacGyver. His face was so covered in blood that Sere started laughing. He looked like a vampire who'd lost all control.

Bart turned to Mr. Fisher. "She's going into shock."

"Fuck shock," Sere said. "Call Kendell. Tell her to bring the van. I'm not going to be able to ride my Triton in this condition."

"In the meantime, what do we do with that body?" Mr. Fisher asked as he pointed a trembling finger at Monty's remains. She hoped she wasn't just imaging that he sounded more like the kindly CPA than the demonic serial killer.

Sere stared hopefully out toward the swamp. From the swath of cleared water hyacinth that was moving her way,

Lefty would be there in a matter of minutes. "I have that covered."

Eventually, the demon's death might still attract the loas of the dead, though without a soul, she wasn't sure how they would respond to Monty's corpse. The only safe place to dispose of him was back in hell, where his body's supernatural molecules would disassociate into nothingness —hopefully taking along with it his memories and intentions.

When Sere's serpent companions slithered ashore, both Bart and Mr. Fisher leaped four feet back toward the trees. They hid even farther into the brush when the thirty-foot alligator cozied up to the shore.

"Holy shit," Bart said. "The Pleistocene gator is real?"

"Maybe next time, you'll treat my boots with more reverence." She turned away from her beloved pet and toward the two men. "It would be best if neither of you ever mentioned his existence. I can't have those brain-dead gator hunters wandering into the deep swamp."

"So we're sharing secrets now?" Bart asked.

She still wasn't fond of putting her trust in anyone, but Bart had proven a useful ally. "I guess you've earned the benefit of the doubt." She watched the two men gather up as much of the bloody, scattered remains as they could, but neither seemed inclined to push the pile of limbs, organs, and tissue closer than six feet from the swamp's shore.

"Just leave it and back away." Sere pulled another shotgun shell from her waistband and scattered the contents from mangled flesh on the water's edge. First to answer her call were her two faithful snakes, but they were quickly joined by a host of their brethren. Together, they worked like a scaly, reptilian conveyor belt, transferring every bit of Monty onto Lefty's back. When no drop of blood was left, Sere dragged her body to the water's edge. Lefty truly looked like a gator from hell with the body remains coating his back. She leaned in close to the giant reptile's head. "Take this shit back to hell."

"I may never leave the city again," Mr. Fisher said.

~

SERE WAS STILL double-checking that she wasn't absorbing some random person's energy when Kendell and Myles emerged from the trees. Kendell ran over and knelt down to smooth the sweaty, swamp-water-smelling, bloodstained hair out of Sere's eyes. "We should have been here with you."

Sere felt like shit, but at least her feelings were all hers and not an amalgam of different inputs. "I couldn't be worrying about you while facing a demon."

Myles helped Mr. Fisher to his feet. "How are you holding up?" Sere could tell from Myles's intensity that he was searching for signs of possession.

"I've been better," the professional businessman said. "It's not every day you meet your demonic double. I'm just glad Sere was able to decapitate the beast before he killed me and got to my family."

"Get him back to the van," Bart said as he hunted around the weeds and grass for anything that might have been left behind.

Mr. Fisher put his arm around Myles's shoulders. He

could barely stand, let alone walk on his own. "Some lunch break."

"Don't worry," Myles said. "We'll take you to Professor Yates's lab. He'll get you back on your feet. Then we'll see about retrieving your Jeep."

Sere leaned in close to Kendell. "Mr. Fisher isn't fully himself. We shouldn't let him out of sight with Myles. It might not be safe."

"We've dealt with possessions a time or two. Myles knows what to look for."

Why does everyone think they know more about hell than I do? Sere thought. "Not like this. Mr. Fisher isn't being controlled by some other spirit. It's a part of him."

"Then we'd best get you back to the van as well." Bart wrapped his strong arms around Sere's legs and torso and lifted her from the ground as if she were a little girl. His embrace enveloped her like the hammock she slept in on Sanguine's porch. Those peaceful, secluded days on the swamp seemed like a lifetime ago. "You'd have been proud of her," Bart continued to Kendell. "She crept up on the Swamp Strangler like a ninja then dispatched him before he could kill Mr. Fisher."

Sere punched his bulging chest muscle. "I don't need you exaggerating my exploits. I told you before. I don't need a sidekick, and I certainly don't need a raconteur."

"What's that?" Bart asked.

She squinted at him, hoping the snarky attitude would convey through her words. "A traveling minstrel who follows along, singing about the exploits of his brave knight."

"You're making that up."

She wrapped her arms around his neck for stability as he carried her down the path. "Embellishing maybe."

"Well, you never know. I have been told I have a lovely singing voice."

Kendell's lack of response wasn't helping. *This is not some budding romance. You don't have to pretend you're not even there.* As they exited the dense brush, Sere leaned over Bart's broad shoulder toward Kendell. "Can you ride a motorcycle? I don't want to leave my Triton just sitting out here."

Kendell shrugged. "I used to putter that yellow scooter all over town. How different can it be?"

You have to be kidding me. "Just go easy on the throttle, and stick to the back roads."

Bart bent down to lower Sere onto the VW's bench seat. "I'll ride my Ducati and keep her company. She'll be fine."

Kendell looked down the dusty road at the two motorcycles. "First, though, you might want those clothes we lent you. I'll go grab your saddlebags as well."

Sere settled back on the blanket-covered vinyl bench. With Myles in the driver's seat, she was able to talk in private to Mr. Fisher, who sat in the back seat. "I know what's inside you."

"Don't worry about me. A man doesn't reach his midfifties without facing down more than a few inner demons. Besides, I deal with the IRS on a regular basis. Any government agency that goes by a three-letter acronym must come from hell." From the determination in his eyes, she could tell there was resolve behind the forced sense of humor.

"Monty isn't some secret dirty garbage bag of past longing. The desires he's dumped into you would be more like having a dump truck bury you in filth. You might have the upper hand now, but he'll never quit. I want you to know I'll do all that I can to free you. You just need to hang on."

The kindly old CPA's smile had to be one he reserved for people in grave economic straits—a combination of sympathy and partnership. His attitude did inspire confidence. "I have my family to keep me sane. They're all the support I'll ever need. But it will be a pleasure to see you again when you're ready."

hen they pulled up to Professor Yates's lab, Sere saw the two motorcycles already parked alongside the building. *You just couldn't resist pushing Kendell to the limit, could you? Fuck you, Bartender Smooth. That woman can barely ride a motorized bicycle.*

Being the first one out of the building, Bart wasn't even smart enough to try to avoid her wrath. "Looks like your friends have everything ready. Let me help you inside." He reached into the van for her arm.

She pulled it away in disgust. "You were supposed to give Kendell a gentle riding lesson, not turn the trip into another of your fucking competitions. You just can't resist showing the size of your dick, can you?"

Kendell stepped out from behind the mountain of a man. "Don't blame him. I might have instigated the race. That bike of yours is really something. If I didn't think Myles and

Cheesecake would have a fit, I'd consider getting one for myself."

Bart's leather jacket over his bare chest gave off the familiar crunching sound as he crossed his arms in satisfaction. "Anytime you want a real lesson, I'd be happy to offer my services."

Myles revved the VW's engine before shutting it off. "Not while I'm her partner. Kendell has used up her allotment of death-defying activities. Now, someone help Sere inside while I give Mr. Fisher a hand." He turned back to the kindly old man. "Once the professor gives you a quick once-over, I'll drive you home. Then I'll call on a friend to help me retrieve your Jeep."

"After this, I may take the afternoon off," Mr. Fisher said. The CPA's seersucker suit, which just a day before had been white and characteristically New Orleans, now looked like it was made out of dirty dishrags.

Sere reached across the seat and took the man's hand. "I was serious. I owe you, and I won't rest until I make it right."

"First, take care of yourself, darlin'. You'll know where to find me when you come up with a cure."

She hobbled off the seat and fell onto the floor of the old VW. Bart loomed over her as if waiting for her to request his help. *Fat chance.*

"Oh, for the love of Pete. You two are like kindergarteners." Kendell leaned down under Sere's shoulder and helped her to her feet before turning on Bart. "Get her other arm. She's not going to ask, and she's not going to swoon over you like some sex-starved romantic.

228

You're just going to have to do it because it's the decent thing."

He took the other shoulder, walking hunched over to allow Sere's feet to remain on the ground. "It's not like I haven't tried."

Kendell shook her head next to Sere's. "Next you're going to say, 'She started it.' In case you haven't already figured it out, Sere's pretty good at taking care of herself. If you want to be in her life, it'd be best to let her take the lead."

If Sere could have bent her neck far enough, she would have kissed Kendell on the cheek for standing up for her. Instead, she felt her legs give out from under her. The two carried her in like a limp doll and laid her out on Professor Yates's metal worktable. She regained full alertness when Polly pulled the technology-enhanced bandage so tightly around her abdomen that she thought her breasts were about to explode out of her bra.

"I don't need any fucking connection."

"The hell you don't," Polly said. "Your side is peeling away like bark off a termite-eaten stump. Now shut up, and let us work."

With Bart and Kendell standing on each side of the table —and Professor Yates and Polly dialing in the equipment— Sere knew she was facing a losing battle. She stared into Bart's smoky brown eyes. *Great. Now not only has he seen me naked, but he also expects to witness me at my weakest and most vulnerable.*

"You should leave now," she said.

Bart crossed his powerful arms in a stance Sere was

getting to know far too well. "I'm not going anywhere. You remember that conversation we had about trust? This is what that looks like."

"Really? I don't think I like it very much." The crackling sound and sparky sensation around her wounds soothed her into unconsciousness.

~

JENNIFER NEARLY BURNED her hand as she reached into the stove for the glass casserole dish. "Ouch."

"You okay, honey?"

She pulled the oven mitt off the counter and slipped it over her hand. "Yeah. I just got momentarily distracted. Dinner's ready, and please turn off the news. I don't want Bobby having nightmares again tonight." Though she'd never admit it to Henry, their son wasn't the only one suffering from sleepless nights.

Locked into the scene like a performer thrust on stage without seeing the script, Sere wanted to bolt for the door. *When the hell did I become June Fucking Cleaver?*

Jennifer's husband, ever the attentive spouse, grabbed a bottle of wine from the fridge and filled her glass before taking his seat at the head of the table. Jennifer favored him with a smile of mutual understanding and took a sip.

The overly sweet taste made Sere wince. *What the hell this shit?* She caught sight of the label. *Chardon-fuckin'-nay? You have to be kidding me. That's barely even alcohol.*

Jennifer set the glass back on the table. "I think this bottle might have gone bad."

"I'll fetch another from the pantry."

She touched his hand before he was able to get up from the table. "No need. I think I'd like to try your Merlot."

"Really? I thought you said it tasted like blood."

She shrugged as if not fully remembering her distaste for the wine. "Tonight it appeals to me."

Bobby came flying in from the hallway like a wild animal and crashed into more than sat in his chair.

"Did you wash your hands, young man?"

He looked at his palms—a sure giveaway that he thought he could pull a fast one on her. "More or less."

"Go wash up. We're having crawfish casserole with green beans."

Yuck! Sere watched in disbelief as Jennifer's well-manicured hands fumbled with the serving knife. Amazingly, she managed to dump the creamy glop onto the plate and not the white-linen tablecloth.

"Looks wonderful, darling," the husband said.

Sere could feel Jennifer's love for the oaf. With any little compliment from the man, her stomach went all fluttery like a foolish schoolgirl's.

For a moment, Sere considered reaching under the woman's dress for the knife that should have been strapped to her thigh. *So this is how societally normal housewives go on killing rampages.* The pain in Sere's side became so intense that Jennifer dropped the serving knife, held her stomach, and leaned over the dining table.

～

"GET THIS FUCKING THING OFF ME!" Sere grabbed the edge of the metal worktable, hoping to hold onto her version of reality.

"It's not done yet." As usual, Professor Yates was more intent on his dials and readouts than on Sere's suffering.

She reached around her stomach and started pulling at the fastener. "*I'm* done." Yanking the wire-impregnated ace bandage off her ribs, she saw the black dots where the pellets had entered her flesh.

"I was afraid of that," the professor said. "Those marks are going to take a lot more work to heal. Without a much longer hookup to Jennifer, they might not ever fade away."

She took a quick glance around the room to make sure Myles had already left with Mr. Fisher. "I've told you before. Call her my *real*. I don't want to ever hear that name."

Polly put her hand on the old scientist's shoulder. "Let Sere decide for herself how much she needs."

Sere ran her hand over the dozen pockmarks on her side. "Leave them. I'll get a tattoo of a flowering vine to camouflage the damage. They'll remind me to be more careful next time."

"Careful isn't your style." Joe's voice made Sere squirm onto her wounds in order to look at him standing in the front entry.

"You're late, old man," she said playfully.

He dropped his black motorcycle helmet and dual saddlebags on Professor Yates's big lounge chair before removing the heavy leather jacket. "I've told you repeatedly not to rely on me, or anyone, to come to your rescue."

She didn't mean to look at Bart, but once she locked her

gaze onto his bulging chest muscles, she found it hard to turn away. "I was getting along just fine on my own. I just thought you might want to see me in action." She used the excuse of trying to sit up as her reason for staring at the man's physique.

"She was pretty impressive with those knives," Bart said.

Joe rubbed a spot on his arm where Sere had jabbed him years ago during a training exercise. "I don't doubt it." Joe came up to the table as Bart stepped aside. "And yet, here you are, getting an energy infusion again. How did Monty get the better of you?"

After every major conflict, Joe always wanted to rehash what she'd done wrong, even when she'd won. She sat with her hands on the edge of the table, accepting the criticism and performing the self-analysis. "I lost my spatial awareness. I should have realized he had fallen on the shotgun. I also got cocky with my assassin pirouette. If I'd landed on him the instant he escaped my grasp, he wouldn't have had time to respond. I keep thinking I've got more time than I actually do. If I'd pinned him to the ground, that would have given Bart enough time to approach with the shotgun and finish him off." *Then Mr. Fisher wouldn't have been infected with Monty the demon.* Some self-incriminations were better kept to herself.

"When you're feeling up to it, we'll set up a training cage in the shipping container. Then we can move on to more open-air-battle techniques. Fighting in real life is different from training in hell."

No shit. Anytime Joe made concessions for her condition, Sere knew he was goading her. "Just let me get some clothes on, and I'll be ready to ride. We can start training in the morning."

"The hell you will, young lady," Kendell said. "You need to rest." She seldom played the protective maternal card, and she didn't pull it off well.

Sere pulled the sides of Myles's old dress shirt around her chest, more to hide her wounds than her bra, which—between the swim in the swamp, the fight, and the shotgun blast—hadn't fared well. "Taking time to rest only puts me behind. Joe's right. My reflexes, awareness, and instincts aren't sharp enough now that I'm here among the living. I'm fine if I can set the fight parameters like in a bar, but out in the open, I get overwhelmed with possibilities. That's only half of my problem, though. Monty snuck out of hell, and I'm afraid others will follow. He had me at a disadvantage from the start. If it hadn't been for Joe's training, he would have completed his mission of killing Montgomery Fisher."

Bart stood behind Joe with his chin in the air as if he expected to be acknowledged as well. *You want a fucking gold star for interfering?* she thought. But then, he had saved her life. "You had your uses too."

She turned to Professor Yates, who still had his arm in a sling from his own encounter with Monty. "Something's bothering me. Why didn't it work?"

"What are you talking about?"

The shotgun marks hurt, but she was once again in full control of her mind. "Why am I still here? I thought that special buckshot was supposed to make me dissolve into nothingness."

Professor Yates picked up the bowl of bloody pellets

Bart had dropped off. "First, you only got hit by one shell, and you didn't even take all of the buckshot. Still, these half dozen stones might have done the job if it weren't for your second advantage, which is the fact that you are not simply a doppelgänger. You have a soul that connects you directly to life. Jen—sorry, your real's projection into hell gives you substance, and that got jumbled. Your spirit was the stabilizing force that kept you grounded."

She wanted to ask about Monty's ability to jump into Mr. Fisher, or what had happened with Thomas after she chopped off his doppelgänger's head years before, but she didn't dare scare everyone else with the demon possessions that she'd inadvertently caused.

Sere hopped down from the table and tested her legs. Her muscles quivered as if she'd just completed an intense training session. Everyone was looking at her. "If you'll all excuse me, I think I'd like to get cleaned up and change."

Joe picked up one of his saddlebags from the floor and handed it to her. "Make one joke about me doing your laundry, and these will be the last leathers I'll repair for you."

❧

SERE COULDN'T BELIEVE it was really her image reflected in the dingy full-length mirror in Professor Yates's laboratory bathroom. Her hair lay plastered against her forehead and neck as if someone had dumped a gallon of glue over her. Rivulets of dried blood covered her from head to toe, the most dramatic being those that trailed down from the half dozen buckshot holes in her side. She turned sideways to inspect the damage. Small black spider veins snaked out from the black pockmarks.

Peeling off the remains of her clothing came as a relief. She stepped into the small shower that was designed for emergency decontamination. *I suppose that's still fitting.* Cold water streamed over her body and mixed with the blood, swamp water, and sweat before running into the metal drain at her feet. It wasn't Kendell's luxury tub of fragrant swirling water, but then, Sere wasn't that type of girl. She lifted her face to be stung by the high-velocity icy gush of water. The pain felt good and invigorating.

When she stepped out of the yellow plastic-draped enclosure, dried off, and looked in the mirror again, the image was that of a woman reborn. Like a kid on Christmas morning, she opened Joe's sack and yanked out every piece of clothing. Among the man's many hidden talents was his ability to work leather into anything from a thick, rough harness to thin, smooth riding pants. She slipped into the tight-fitting pants and halter top that reacted to her every movement like a second layer of skin. Sheathing her knife next to her leg in the alligator boots completed her transformation into the badass demon hunter.

When she rejoined the others, she noticed her shotguns lying on the worktable. Joe was finishing up his cleaning and reassembly of the weapons. "How did these work out for you?"

She ran her hand over the tender scars. "The single-barrel might be useful in slowing down human or demon, but it won't finish the job. I need to keep the four-barrel more easily accessible."

As if reading her mind, he reached into his remaining saddlebag and tossed her a leg holster and bullet belt loaded with shells. "These will make you considerably more obvious in your intentions, but you won't have to fish around the back of your riding jacket for the butt of the gun, and you'll have your ammunition on you."

Sere fastened the leather straps around her waist and leg then holstered the shotgun at her thigh. "I'm not hiding who I am any longer. I am the devil's daughter, and it's my job to return hell's demons to their rightful realm."

Bart handed her the leather riding jacket. "In that case, I guess we'll all have our work cut out for us."

BOOK LIST

Other Stories
Through the Lens

ABOUT THE AUTHOR

G.A. Chase is the pen name for Greg Chase. He is a science fiction and paranormal author living in New Orleans with his wife, fellow author Deanna Chase, and their two shih tzu dogs. On any given day you can find him behind his computer, people watching in the Quarter, or out in his studio creating stories in glass. His glass work can be found at www.chase-designs.com.

www.gregchaseauthor.com